Aflame Books
2 The Green
Laverstock
Wiltshire
SP1 1QS
United Kingdom
email: info@aflamebooks.com

ISBN: 9781906300043
First published in 2009 by Aflame Books

This translation is published by arrangement
with NB Publishers, South Africa

First published in Afrikaans as *Mahala,*
by Tafelberg Uitgewers, Cape Town, 1972.

British Library Cataloguing in Publication Data
A catalogue record for this book is available from the British Library

Cover design by Zuluspice: www.zuluspice.com

Printed in Turkey

MAHALA

CHRIS BARNARD

TRANSLATED BY LUZETTE STRAUSS

For Elsa and Klaas

1

Fear had been part of him for so long that he no longer recognised it as fear. It was in his careful, almost skulking manner of walk; in his restless, mistrustful eyes, in his unusually soft voice; in his oft-stammering manner of talking.

He seldom reminded himself that he had to be careful, had to keep his eyes peeled. It had long been habit that he would rather not meet strangers, that he would only go to Caipemba if it was absolutely essential. The noise and frivolity of bars irritated him. Strangers bored him. People tired him out. But he no longer related any of these things to fear.

So he had not been thinking of Ritter that afternoon when the girl suddenly spoke to him. He only knew that he wanted to get rid of her; because someone, he thought – anyone – must be careful of a girl who accosts you in the street. Even if she barely looks sixteen. Even if she looks innocent and very unsure of herself.

He was way ahead of his shadow heading back to the river. The boat would leave in a quarter of an hour. The afternoon was sharp and hot and his shirt clung wetly to his back. Then he saw her jump down from the veranda of a shop and head for him, between the flies and the blacks' fruit baskets. She was skinny and quite short, a little forlorn in her sweaty dress. Her shoulders were naked and brown from the sun and her hair, cut short, tied behind her head with a ribbon.

"*Senhor*," she said, "do you know when the boat leaves?"

"The packet?" he asked and stood expectantly.

"*Faz favor.*"

"In quarter of an hour."

They both stared at the boat momentarily where it rested two hundred paces away against the riverbank, behind the green and quivering corrugated iron sheds. Then she asked, without looking at him: "Do you know how much it costs?"

"To where?"

"To the third stop."

That is when he got a fright. And the fear made him irritatingly aware of the flies around his hot face and of the prickly sun. He wanted to shake her off and get on to the boat and get a seat behind the gauze, in the shade.

"Twenty-four escudos," he said and began walking.

"*Senhor*," she said urgently behind him. "*Faz favor...*"*

He stood, but did not look at her.

The third stop was his. And only he had ever got off there. Only he and sometimes, very seldom, someone from the coffee farm. But she was a stranger.

She came to stand beside him again and he could see how she took a handkerchief out of the front of her dress and held it out to him. "My money was in here. I lost it."

He was tired and there were flies in the sun around her face. There were flies everywhere. The afternoon was a listless and monotonous buzzing of flies and bees and the air smelled of brown mango blossoms and the sweet stench of fermenting palm fronds.

She was carrying a black leather bag. It was hanging at her hip on a strap that crossed over her shoulder. The strap cut a furrow between her small round breasts, from left to right. She put her hand into the bag and briefly scratched around in it. "I don't have much here, *senhor*," she said, "but if you help me, you can have this bag. It's a new bag. I'll take all the stuff out."

Rodrigues stood in the cool shade of the gangplank, but his eyes moved towards the girl and stayed with her.

"I'll pay for the two of us, Rodrigues," Delport said.

The girl's bag swung somewhat self-consciously at her knees while he counted the money out.

He hoped she would go and sit somewhere else, but she followed him right into the corner and sat next to him against the

* Senhor – Sir; Faz favor – Please.

As this novel is set in Mozambique the lingua franca would be Portuguese.

wire gauze, her bag on her lap. She was wet from sweat and there were large stains under her arms.

Being in the shade was good. But outside the ilala palms reverberated against the grey air and Delport closed his eyes and listened to the racket of the cluster of ducks on the top deck and the blacks talking loudly out in the white heat and Rodrigues standing lazily and counting change. On board, enclosed in wire gauze, it was cooler and he felt the boat rocking slightly in the current, and somewhere the anchor rope creaked and he was glad to know the day was over. He would be able to sit and sleep until the third stop and by then the sun would already have set and he would walk home up the incline, between the mango trees and the banana trees, and he would drink his whisky outside on the veranda and smell the night.

It was always good to be back on the boat after a day like that and to listen to Rodrigues and to head downstream into the afternoon, through the green bush, to welcome the night, with the blacks on the top deck chatting and laughing and sometimes singing unaccompanied, with the smell of goat dung and coconuts and garlic, and Rodrigues picking his teeth and calmly sitting and talking and smelling of brandy. And a goat intermittently bleating on the top deck, and the monotonous thud of the engine that sometimes became a double beat as the bank neared and the sound bounced back over the green water.

All this was good after such a day, because it would be cooler and the sun would be gone, and all these things, all the smells and sounds, would mean that he would not see Caipemba again for at least four weeks.

The girl shuffled closer to him and he peered through slit eyes in the hope that he would see her walking away, but vaguely he saw her two brown knees and knew she was still sitting next to him. She must have noticed his eyes opening, because she spoke again.

"Are you getting off before the third stop?" she asked.

He shook his head.

"Where are you getting off?"

He opened his eyes completely and looked up, but not at her, and said: "At the third stop."

He closed his eyes again and leant his head back against the wire mesh and smelled the quay's dust. He wanted to forget about this girl and make her understand it, but at the same time he knew he would not be able to forget about her before he knew where she was going. It would be dark when they disembarked and the nearest roof, apart from the one he would be able to offer, was twelve kilometres from the river.

Then the boat's whistle sounded outside.

He could hear how the blacks began talking more animatedly and someone was busy dragging a white goat on a sisal rope up the gangplank. The goat's hooves scratched rowdily over the wood.

"How long does it take to get to the third stop?" she asked.

This time he looked at her. "Three hours."

Now he saw her face properly for the first time. There were fine droplets of sweat under her nose and on her forehead, and her eyes were a little too large. "It'll be dark," she said.

He nodded.

The whistle sounded again and Rodrigues was busy pulling the gangplank up. Then the boat suddenly began vibrating and a moment later the engine stuttered into life, gasped a few times and then found its rhythm.

All his attention was on the quay. He saw a row of black children waving and on the top deck some shouted their final messages to the shore. Pio was busy untying the anchor rope and the current began to catch. Then, very slowly, the corrugated iron buildings began to slide away and black children's faces became smaller and were swinging away from him.

Then they were free in the current, drifting and on course, the engine's thud deeper and suddenly regular.

Farewell Caipemba, he thought, and wondered when Rodrigues would be coming past. But Rodrigues was busy somewhere. He could hear him talking with the helmsman and the air was sweet with mango blossoms and dried fish and he thought again: Farewell.

The child would be playing: somewhere in the shade of the mango trees he would be driving tins and cotton reels on roads he had scraped clear in the sand with a piece of wood, on one of the many roads that were everywhere in the backyard, from shadow to shadow, weaving roads that forked left and right over the wide plot and turned and doubled back and always somehow ended at the same place.

The child would be playing and Ann would be sleeping under the safety of her mosquito net in her musty room with the walls made of planks – walls from which the whitewash was flaking off, walls with blisters and cracks and fine brown dots of cockroach dung. Walls of riddles and silences and ecstasy.

Ann would be sleeping or lying and staring at the ceiling where geckos slept motionless against the cornice.

They would not miss him.

Behind the boat the churned up water lay like a ruffled fin and he could only just see the tops of Caipemba's palm trees and a row of white egrets coming over the bush and flying silently by.

Then he heard Rodrigues coming down the steps.

There was a matchstick between his teeth and his hands were black with dry oil. "Hi," he said and addressed himself to the girl. "My name is Rodrigues. Captain Rodrigues Pereira." She did not mind his dirty hand offered in greeting; she was apparently relieved to find someone willing to talk.

"Mália Domingo," she said.

"Where are you heading?" He went to sit on the other side of her.

"I'm going as far as the third stop."

"Oh yes, you and Max are together." When she did not immediately grasp it, he nodded towards Delport.

She shook her head. "No. I'm at a hunting camp next to Dois creek. My father and a friend of his came hunting and I'm looking after the camp."

"Big game?"

"They're looking for elephant and buffalo. But they've been gone for a week. They should have been back by now."

Rodrigues spat his matchstick out and took a new one out of his matchbox. "How did you get to Caipemba? You weren't on the boat on our way down yesterday?"

She hesitated for a moment. But only for a moment. And in that moment she looked at Delport. They looked each other straight in the eye and he could see the hesitation; then she turned her head away and looked again at Rodrigues. "Someone took me. One of the people from the coffee plantation."

"Do you know people there?" Rodrigues wanted to know.

"No." She drew her leather bag closer to her chest. "We don't know anyone."

"I wish more people would come hunting here," the captain said and laughed in Delport's direction. Then he looked again at the girl, the laughter still around his mouth, but his eyes unsure, in search of Mália Domingo's reaction. "There's no women around here. Two or three married ones in Caipemba. And two or three at CCG. And Max's wife. Max is one of the lucky ones."

Delport waited on the next sentence, but it would not come. He had expected the captain to say: "I've never been married." He often said it. Delport had been around a hundred times before when he had said it. And it was always with exactly the same intonation in his voice and the same expression in his eyes. He always said it as someone would say: "I've got cancer."

That first night, nine years ago, he had heard it for the first time. The night he had met Rodrigues Pereira. They had waited the entire afternoon in Caipemba, he and Ann, for the boat to depart. But they could only leave at ten o'clock, because they were still waiting for someone. It was ten o'clock at night and it was oppressive and they were on the move – without the one they had been waiting for. And Rodrigues came to sit with them and talked to them about the stars like an old friend talks about shared secrets. Rodrigues was a bit drunk that night and he had told them his whole life story. But what Delport could remember most clearly was the way in which Rodrigues suddenly said: "I've never been married."

"Are you from Beira?" the captain asked and the girl nodded. He took a half-smoked cheroot out of the top pocket of his uniform and, deep in thought, lit it. "Nice place. Beira. I was there for a while. At the docks. That was before I became captain here."

The rank only existed in his imagination. Perhaps that is why he was so attached to it. He always added the rank when he introduced himself to a stranger. And the threadbare uniform was, nevertheless, covered in medals that he got from who-knows-where – perhaps from the pawn shops in Beira and Porto Amélia.

Delport sat and listened. He knew all the stories already – the stories of Rodrigues's days in Beira, and of the girlfriend he had there, and how she had been in a tragic accident one Sunday afternoon in November. But it was good to hear him telling it again, these stories: with suitably comforting words from Gibran and the Rig Veda and the Song of Solomon.

He sat and listened to Rodrigues and thought about Ann, who was apparently his wife, and about the child who would play alone in the yard and almost never slept at night.

"You remain a lodger," he heard Rodrigues say. "You remain a lodger. As soon as you set foot here, it's over for you. This here is Africa and Africa is merciless. Africa feels sorry for no one. Portugal was different."

Pio called from the engine room, but Rodrigues first finished smoking his cheroot before he took notice of Pio. He sucked on his cheroot until it burnt down to his thumbnail, then stamped it out under his heel and stood up. "The blacks," he said "can't do anything unless you watch over them. The diesel's probably leaking again."

Then they were alone again. Delport and the girl. All that remained of the captain was a brief puff of his cheroot smoke. But Delport was already more relaxed, not so wary, and he waited for her to talk. He suddenly wanted her to start talking.

But she did not. Not immediately.

The thud of the engine was a hidden but comforting noise somewhere beneath the surface of the water. He could feel the noise through the soles of his shoes. The sun was disappearing and behind them, on the horizon, the sky was grey and purple as if there might be rain that night.

On the top deck one of the black children cried and a woman's voice drowsily admonished the child. The goats and poultry were calmer than usual, but now and again a white or grey down feather would waft right past Delport's face and float down to the water and settle on the current.

When he looked again, the girl was busy emptying her black leather bag. In front of her feet there was already a packet of sugar and a cake of soap, a tube of toothpaste, a new bottle of perfume, a tin of salt. He sat and watched how she unpacked what remained: a magazine, two paperbacks, and something wrapped up in newspaper that sounded like wood when she put it down.

When the bag was empty, she put it down next to Delport. "The bag, *senhor*."

"Why did you empty it?" he wanted to know.

"The bag's for you. For the boat fare."

"Keep the bag," he said. "I don't want it."

"You'll make me feel better if you take it."

"Keep it," he said. "Put your stuff away. Anyway, how are you going to carry it without a bag?"

She began pushing the stuff on the floor to one side. "I'll be perfectly alright."

He squatted down and pulled the bag closer and began putting the stuff back again, without saying anything. She tried to stop him. "*Senhor*," she said, but he kept on putting it back. As he picked up the thing wrapped in newspaper, he tore the paper and a piece of wood fell between them. It was oval and hollowed out like a plate. He wanted to pick it up, but she was faster than him. She picked it up carefully and turned her back.

"Is it damaged?" he wanted to know.

"No," she said after a moment. "Thankfully not." And then laughed relieved and turned to show him. "It's beautiful, don't you think? I bought it for eighty escudos."

He looked up into the two hollow eyes. It was a mask, of the sort sold by the Indians in Caipemba, carved from the wood of a wild olive tree. He stared into the two hollow eyes, for a second, and then he saw the nose, and then the wide cheekbones, and then the mouth that turned down slightly at the corners. And something seemed vaguely familiar. He looked at the eyes under the heavy eyebrows again, and for a moment felt as if he couldn't breathe, but then the feeling was gone and a strange shiver ran down his neck and over his shoulders and over his stomach down to his legs.

"Don't you like it?" the girl asked. "I think it's wonderful. It was carved with a pocketknife and it only cost eighty escudos!"

He nodded and looked away. A white feather wafted past his face again. And the child was no longer crying. It was dead quiet and the thudding of the engine carved the silence into equal-sized chunks.

The girl was still holding the mask for him, but he was no longer looking. Because the face was Ritter's and he did not want to look at it.

Ritter stood at the door and his eyes were as dead as the wood in Mália Domingo's hands. He stood at the door, his one hand on the wire gauze and the other in the pocket of his khaki bush jacket. The room smelled of the sweet perspiration of thatch and of Ann who was still lying on the bed. He did not want to do it. He had no intention of doing it, but when he remembered the glass in his hand, he threw his arm back and the glass flew through the air and broke in Ritter's face and the next moment he was in the kitchen next to the cold stove and then outside in the rain.

That was the second time he had run away like a coward and the last time he had seen Ritter.

"What's wrong?" the girl asked. "Don't you feel well?"

That night they had slept at a stranger's house in Empangeni, outside Durban. And the whole night he had waited in vain for Ritter.

Nine years is a long time if you must pass it day by day. Nine years is a long time if you are waiting, and even longer if you wait in the wilderness. But if you look back, it is a fleeting moment – the moment when you blinked.

Somewhere in the distance the girl was talking about the sun. But her voice disappeared and he brought his hands to his face and pressed them against his temples. And her voice returned and he heard her asking if she could get him a drink of water.

He shook his head and said: "No thanks."

It is not the mask, he thought suddenly. Perhaps the similarity is not that great. It was just that moment of clarity when he suddenly remembered Ritter's face again. Ritter stood at the door and they were his eyes and he remembered everything again and felt everything again and knew clearly once again that he still awaited him. And that was it – that knowledge. Because sometimes he was convinced that he had outgrown the fear; that he no longer waited; that he had made peace with himself. But at that moment he knew more clearly than ever that it was not so. And that made him feel faint.

He could smell the girl's hair and that was the first time in a very long time that he had smelled a woman again – a woman's hair and a woman's skin. The girl was once again in the half light in front of him and he saw her suntanned shoulders and he remembered her name.

The sun had now gone down.

To the left and the right the water lay green and dark and there were no longer any egrets, but somewhere against the wire gauze a mosquito sang monotonously and disappeared and buzzed back, flew around his face and disappeared.

"I like the mask," he said eventually. "Did you buy it in Caipemba?"

"Yes."

"Where?"

"Just on the pavement. There was a blind Indian sitting and his baskets were full of carvings – masks and animals carved from wood, and wooden beads, and stuff from ivory."

"Why did you buy this mask?" he asked.

"I liked it. It was different from all the other faces. It was a European face."

"I like it," he said. "I'd really like to buy it from you. I'll give you a hundred escudos – then you can make a profit."

She didn't answer.

"I collect masks," he said. "I've already got about twenty or so. This one is something special."

She was not very willing; that much he could see. She smiled uncertainly, picked the mask up and looked at it. "You're making it difficult for me, *senhor*," she said. "I already owe you some money. I should have given it to you as a present, but..." She laughed unconvincingly and briefly and ran her hand over the wooden face. "It's so beautiful. I really wanted to keep it."

"It is something remarkable," he said again. "It will fit right in with the others I have." He looked at her. "A hundred and fifty escudos, *senhora*."

"Please," she said, and it was almost as if she were begging. "I would really like to keep it."

It was that moment between afternoon and the evening when the darkness grew almost visibly. He could no longer see her face all that clearly, he could only just make out the shadows of her eyes and her nose and mouth. They sat in the darkness looking at each other.

"You're making me feel guilty," she said, "but you can take the leather bag. It's new and it's worth more than the mask."

Suddenly, out of the silence, the boat's whistle sounded breathlessly and it was a lonely sound on the wide-open water. On the top deck chickens began clucking and a turkey gobbled anxiously.

"I don't want anything for nothing," he said. "I wanted to buy the mask."

To their right the bank was now much closer and he stood up.

"Why is the whistle going off?" she asked.

He looked through the wire gauze until he could see the lanterns and then turned to face where she still sat holding the mask. He already knew where he would hang it: inside on the wall right under the buffalo head. He smiled and said: "We're at the first stop."

Pio came in with his shuffling step and lit the oil lamp and suddenly it was completely dark outside. Some of the blacks were busy disembarking. Several were not carrying anything; others had baskets with fruit and groceries and dried fish balancing on their heads; others struggled to get cages, carrying chickens and ducks and other poultry, down the gangplank. Only once all those who wanted to get off had done so did Rodrigues take up his position on the bank and collect fares from new passengers. There was a lantern burning near his head and he was wet with sweat in his heavy and threadbare uniform. He intermittently slapped a wayward beetle or moth away from his face and then moved a little further away from the lantern.

Delport surprised himself by getting into a conversation with the girl. She asked him something about Rodrigues and he was busy telling her everything he knew about the captain. It suddenly gave him a sense of excitement that he could not quite grasp. He was busy sitting and talking to a stranger in the dark and he couldn't remember when last that had happened.

And while he talked, he was thinking: it's strange that I should do it now, right after being reminded again of him. Something told him that perhaps he was over the fear; he was no longer afraid; Ritter was someone in another world. Ritter was dead.

He thought of Rodrigues's words from a few months previously. They were sitting in the bridge on their way to Caipemba that morning and Rodrigues was drunk and garrulous. Rodrigues said, while sitting and cleaning his fingernails with a matchstick: "The river is the safest place in Africa, *amo*. It's neither here nor there. It's somewhere between two sides." He flicked the broken matchstick away and sniffed and picked up his brandy. "While you're on the river, you're nowhere. You're drifting in nothingness, like Nietzsche or someone or other said. You're just an idea."

While he was thinking about it, he told it to the girl, without knowing if she understood, and without worrying one way or the other. "He's strange," she said. "He asked me so many questions."

"He questions everybody like that. He knows everything about every white person on his boat. He considers it his job to know everything about everyone." Then he used João's words. "He lives through other people. Perhaps because he never lived himself."

"It must be a boring job," she said, "always going back and forth. The same river. Every day."

And somewhere in the past he heard Rodrigues confirming. "That's right. I'm in transit. Always. Do you know what I'm saying? Every day is yesterday in reverse. And the day after tomorrow is just like today." Back and forth, four times a week, between Caipemba and Schwulst's small thatched-roof hotel at Lotsumo – the fifth stop.

On the top deck, someone was busy feeling their way over the stiff twanging keys of an mbira. It was an airy sound in the balmy darkness, but sweet and beautifully circular and, apart from the goat, everyone up there was listening. The goat bleated now and again. And that reminded Delport of the fever trees at Mkuze and the man with the sores at Catuane who gave Ann his dead wife's clothes, and the hunger in Moamba when Ann refused to go any

20

further, and the mbira at midday at João Belo which played beneath their green hotel room window as the sun went down and settled over a desolate world.

He longed for Ann, because she was no longer with him. The pale face under the mosquito net was lifeless.

João had also fled. Rodrigues as well. João ran away from a woman who wanted to love him and Rodrigues from a debacle. But João and Rodrigues were content with that – they had said so themselves. He would also be able to, if Ann had only stayed the same.

The girl's head rested against the wire gauze and he looked at her and asked: "Are you tired?" And thought: I am so used to asking that question!

"It's so humid," she said. "Can't we go upstairs?"

"No one will stop you," he said.

He did not want to go, but when she waited, he stood up and followed her. They went up the wooden stairs to the top deck and he went to stand next to her. There was a wooden railing around the deck, and people were leaning against the railings and looking out over the river. Others sat together in huddles, around their baskets and poultry. The goat stood aimlessly at the end of its rope and stared into the darkness.

"It's cooler here," she said.

They walked between the people sitting on deck, climbed over the baskets and bundles and cages made of chicken-wire. The thudding of the engine was more distinct now and Delport could see the funnel against the stars and the puffs of smoke rising into the darkness.

"This is the first time that I've ever been on a riverboat like this," she said. "It's just like I imagined it would be."

The mbira still twanged somewhere in the darkness and languid voices could be heard here and there. The day had taken its toll.

"You're married?" she asked.

He could smell pineapples and chicken droppings and garlic.

"Yes," he said and nodded.

Ann would probably be sleeping already. Or lying down and reading.

"Children?"

They went to the front railing and leant over, stood and watched how the bow cut the current open. "One," he said.

"How old?"

They had not come to the islands yet. That would be in another quarter of an hour. Then the second stop. He wondered what had happened to his bearer. He couldn't see him in the dark.

"Nine," he said, "about," and did not appreciate her inquisitiveness. He would much rather go and sit and chat with Rodrigues.

"Is it a boy?"

He nodded without making sure that she had seen it.

"It must be lonely," she said, "for a child."

"For everyone."

The night was sticky and motionless and even the boat's passage brought no relief. The two words remained hanging in the air and he couldn't grasp what had made him say that. It was his own problem, after all.

"I'm only here for two weeks," she said, "and the loneliness kills me. Sometimes I feel as if I can't breathe. That's why I went to Caipemba yesterday. I just wanted to see some people again."

His eyes searched for his bearer among the dark shapes. But he couldn't see him.

"You told Rodrigues you've been here for one week," he said softly.

She lifted her eyes up from the water, looked at him and turned away, and, like him, leant with her back against the railing. "A week in the camp. We came from Beira two weeks ago."

Could Gonçalo have missed the boat? It had happened before. But never with that servant. Gonçalo was always the most reliable of the lot.

"You're not allowed hunting here," he said.

"My dad has permits."

"I didn't sign them."

She looked up at him somewhat uncertainly. "Are you a game warden?"

He nodded. "Actually a fire warden. But I have to keep an eye on everything. They should have brought the permits to me first."

"They didn't know that."

"The licensing office in Beira would have told them. And it's printed on the back of the permit."

"I'll tell them," she said, an edge of concern in her voice, "when they come back – if they come. I'll tell them to come straight to you. They definitely don't want to cause any trouble."

For a moment there was a bond between them, the possibility of a bond, the vague promise of a relationship – the way in which she had said it – if they come.

Someone else, he wondered, standing at the point of being left in the lurch? Someone else, he almost hoped, who has lost all sense of security? He looked directly into her face, for the second time that day, and asked: "Is there a possibility they won't come back?"

"They've been gone for a week already," she said. "They were only going to go for four days."

Delport thought of Ann for a moment, consciously defenceless in her crumpled petticoat, standing at the stove and watching Fernando fry two eggs – her thin and sagging body ten years older than her years.

Somebody came up the stairs and Delport looked and saw Rodrigues's cap appear, and then his round shoulders. His heavy frame swayed up the stairs and came to a standstill at the top. He did not notice the two of them immediately and took his pipe out, put it slowly into his mouth, felt around in his pockets for matches. His head did not move, but in his imagination Delport could see Rodrigues's eyes turning in their sockets in search of them.

"Here we are!" the girl said and Rodrigues looked in their direction. A yellow flame burst into life between his hands and he lit his pipe carefully, flicked the match into the water, sucked on the pipe to make it smoulder well and then approached them.

"Didn't know you were here," he said, but convinced no one, and apparently realised it, and said: "There's a storm on the way."

In the east, a little light stirred, deep behind the clouds; but fleetingly, before everything was covered in darkness again.

"I've just been looking for you two down there," the captain said. "But you weren't there."

"We came to get some fresh air."

Rodrigues sucked valiantly and in vain on his pipe, then searched for his matches again, found them – and apparently forgot why he wanted them.

"I saw the mask that's lying there with your stuff," he said to Delport. "Did you buy it at Rajput's?"

Delport shook his head and nodded towards the girl. "It's hers."

"Bloody nice." He addressed himself to her. "Bloody nice, you know. Unusual sort of face. It reminded me of Shiva."

Neither of them took the trouble to ask who Shiva was.

"And of Janus as well, don't you think? Now that I think about it." Rodrigues weighed up the matter. "There is something of Janus in that face. It's both of his faces together." He waited for someone to react, but neither of them knew who Janus was. And neither wanted to ask.

"Did my bearer come on board this afternoon?" Delport asked.

The captain nodded. "He got on before you did."

They stood uncomfortably in front of each other. There was nothing more to say and yet there was lots more. There would be lots if Delport and Rodrigues were alone, or Rodrigues and the girl or the girl and Delport. But the three of them together were now awkward and a little restless. There was a tension that earlier in the evening had been missing.

Rodrigues lit his pipe for a second time and his face was brown behind the flame, his cheeks shiny with stubble and sweat. "What a night!" he said and flicked his match away. A beam of light shone out from the steps from the deck below and the smoke from his pipe drifted blue through the lightbeam. "What a night!"

It was like any other night on the river. But Rodrigues always wanted to try and avoid the moment with words.

"Will it rain?" the girl asked.

Lightning suddenly flashed in the west as well, quick, like the blink of an eye, and Rodrigues saw it and nodded. "It looks like Umlenzengamunye is running riot again."

"Who?" The girl looked from the captain to Delport.

Rodrigues immediately stood a bit closer. It was the moment he had been waiting for. "Umlenze-nga-munye," he articulated pedantically.

Delport knew: until the second stop, Rodrigues would

mercilessly beat the silence back with tales of an invisible world that he had learnt about on so many thousand solitary river voyages.

"Umlenzengamunye is the name the blacks use for One-Leg."

Delport tried to move off unnoticed.

"It's the lightning that jumps over the earth with one fiery leg," Rodrigues explained. "And One-Leg is the Great-Great One's helper, his messenger."

Delport already knew this story inside out.

"Sometimes Umlenzengamunye comes down to earth in the guise of lightning. Then everyone can see him and be forewarned. And sometimes he comes in the guise of a man, the guise of an old man – but then he appears in the mist and the rain and only women and children can recognise him."

In Rodrigues's small and untidy cabin there was a small bookshelf: books with oil-smeared and dog-eared pages and pencil underlining on every second sentence; pages with unreadable notes in the margins. In this cramped and cluttered cabin he had spent twenty-two years between brandy bottles and books, collecting useless knowledge, only to be able to impart it to the uninitiated who would be too bored not to listen.

Delport climbed between the wire cages and suitcases and baskets and searched in the darkness. "Gonçalo!" he called out half-heartedly. And again after a while – "Gonçalo!" Then someone stood up next to the stairs and raised his white canvas cap respectfully, and Delport recognised the bearer.

He went past Gonçalo and climbed down the stairs to the deck below. His skin itched from mosquito bites and the day's sweat and it was suddenly humid again among the lanterns. Pio stood behind the helm and picked his nose and Delport walked past him to the bench in the stern where he and Mália Domingo had sat earlier. The leather bag was still on the floor and on the bench he saw the mask lying face down.

There was a moment during which he hesitated, but then he bent over and picked the mask up and turned it face up. The wood was heavy and shiny and dark like Rodrigues's face when he lit his pipe. But it was Ritter looking up at him, and he closed his eyes and saw Ritter standing at the screendoor with his one hand in the pocket of his bush jacket. His hair was wet from the rain and his eyes deep in their sockets and he wanted to say: it's not my fault, for god's sake, it's nobody's fault – but the room was still sweet from Ann's body and shards of glass glittered in the light as they broke against Ritter's forehead.

He would put Rodrigues to the test. He would drill a hole through the forehead and hang the mask under the buffalo head and tell Rodrigues about it. He put the mask down and took out his wallet, turned the money out on to his hand, counted it: there was two hundred and fifteen escudos. He would offer her two hundred.

The girl's handkerchief lay on the bench, the one out of which her money had been stolen. He picked it up and instantly he could smell her again. It was a smell he was no longer used to. He folded the handkerchief open and in the one corner letters were embroidered. A. DOM.

Amália Domingo.

He did not feel guilty that he was doing it; for some reason or other he felt she would not mind as he folded the handkerchief up and put it in his shirt pocket. He wanted to carry her smell with him.

The first islands came past. The bare branches were dotted with sleeping egrets and somewhere behind the thudding of the engine, Delport could hear bullfrogs croaking.

He went to stand at the gauze and looked out at the beetles and moths and bugs clinging to the outside, arrested in their blind flight. Some sat quite still, the wings of others vibrated as they crept up the gauze in search of an entrance.

He went to sit on the bench and reached out in the darkness towards the mask, found it, began running his fingertips over it: over the heavy and gaping mouth, over the wide cheeks, the strong eyebrows above the hollows of the eyes. Ritter stood in the witness stand and he sat and watched how the muscles in his jaw worked while he stood and looked unemotionally at the judge – and he hated Ritter because he was scared of him. And he loved him. They came down the stairs and he could hear the wheezing of Rodrigues's breath; he took his hand away from the mask and waited until their faces appeared in the light of the lantern.

"Max," Rodrigues called out, suddenly jovial. "A drink?"

Delport did not feel like a drink with Rodrigues, but he nodded. They went down the narrow stairway into Rodrigues's stuffy, small cabin. It was dark and the captain was searching for his matches. The air was warm and it felt as if the darkness clung stickily to their bodies; the darkness made Delport feel as if he couldn't breathe and he was impatient for Rodrigues to light the lamp. But he was taking his time and constantly mumbling to himself and his breath wheezed and Delport smelled tobacco and the strange, sweet flavour of Mália Domingo's stale eau de cologne.

The light brought no relief. When the lantern was eventually burning, it was even more humid than before. The girl went to sit on the bed and began looking around the room, and Delport's eyes followed her inquisitive gaze: over the writing table with the loose papers and ink pots and worn out Rig Veda, over the shelf with forlorn books, over the half-open wardrobe with the dirty underwear – and eventually to the wall directly opposite her: it was covered right up to the low ceiling with pornographic photos and magazine clippings of models.

"How about a game of chess?" the captain asked. "While we have a drink?"

Delport shook his head. "It'll take too long."

"This guy plays chess well," Rodrigues said to the girl. "When we play, we always play as if our lives depend on it. We always say the guy who loses will be executed at dawn. But Max always wins – and here I am still."

Rodrigues got down on his knees and pulled a chest out from under the bed, took out a full bottle of brandy. "KWV from the Cabo de Boa Esperança," he announced. "Nectar of the gods from the land of the gods!"

That's when he noticed what the girl was looking at. He pushed the chest back under the bed and came groaningly upright. "You don't mind do you?" he asked and pointed with his thumb at the wall. She shook her head. He then put the bottle down on the table among the ink pots, drew two glasses and a mug nearer and began ladling water with the mug from a clay pot on the floor. "Don't think badly of me," he said somewhat embarrassed. "Grant me these few pictures." He turned to look at her. "It's a poor substitute for the real thing, *senhora*, but if the real thing keeps evading you…" He poured the brandy into the water and gave the girl her glass, Delport his and kept the mug for himself, sighed as he sat down, and said: "I've never been married."

The brandy was insipid and tasteless and Delport knew he would never manage to finish it.

Rodrigues suddenly became quiet and so all three of them sat in silence. There was just the regular thudding of the engine and in the open porthole above the bed a disoriented reed moth that intermittently fluttered its green wings.

The boat swayed slightly, very slightly, and that made Delport sway slowly in his chair while he looked at the girls stuck on the wall and thought of Ann and of Mália Domingo. He thought of them and heard the hiss of the lamp and sat and stared at the big lopsided shadow opposite him against the wall; and the shadow nodded in time with him, raised and put down its glass, sat unmoving together with him and waited for the third stop.

Each of them was immersed in their own fermenting thoughts. And they sat like that, sweating, and sipped at their insipid brandy and listened to the thudding of the engine.

Rodrigues's mug was empty first and he poured another for himself. When the second mug was almost empty, he got up and went to get something out of the wardrobe. It was what Delport had anticipated: a large cake tin full of photos from a decaying, godforsaken past.

The photos, like everything Rodrigues possessed, smelled of tobacco. They were, like everything Rodrigues possessed, moth eaten and covered in greasy fingerprints. They were of a thin child standing with his arms stiffly by his sides staring into the sun and laughing proudly at the camera, Lisbon's streets full of cars from the 1930s, a young boy waving from a train window, a man in a sailor's uniform, a sailor standing with his hand around the waist of a thin girl in old-fashioned clothes, a gravestone in Beira, a riverboat.

There was not much. There was barely enough to cover the bottom of the tin. It was unlikely that there would ever be more. In his wardrobe, between the tobacco and underwear, lay a box camera, but as Rodrigues himself had explained once upon a time: "It's been there for almost twenty years, and I never use it. There's nothing more to take photos of."

Rodrigues took the photos from the girl and put them back in the tin, put the tin away – then looked at Delport, self-consciously, not sure what else he could do to impress the girl. "You sure you don't want to play chess?" But before Delport could answer, the captain addressed himself to the girl. "Do you play chess? Don't you perhaps want to play?"

The girl shook her head and suddenly looked tired. "I don't know how," she said.

Rodrigues took the chess board out of the wardrobe and put it in front of her on the table, unfolded it, and began carefully unpacking the pieces.

"Max got it at Rajput's," he said. "The same guy who you bought that mask from. Funny bloke, that Rajput. He introduced me to the Rig Veda. And Tarot cards." He bent over towards the girl, asthmatic and earnest. "They're different from normal chess pieces." The girl took a pawn from him, then a king.

The pieces were made of ivory wood and olivewood. Each pawn was a small mask standing on two thin legs and holding a sword. The ivory wood king was a crowned lion's head, but the mane looked like woven sunbeams. The black olivewood king was the head of a bull with a five-sided crown between its long, curved horns. "Max is always black," the captain said. "I'm always white."

The girl examined the pieces one by one as he gave them to her, and put them down in front of her, one by one, in a row, and then pushed them away from her and looked up at Delport.

"Max and I always play," Rodrigues said. "But he wins every time. He's good. You don't catch him out easily."

The reed moth fluttered its wings again and then suddenly tried to fly, but hit the ceiling, fell to the floor and didn't move.

Delport's hands were clammy on his glass and he could feel how the sweat was beading on his face and running down his temples. He thought of the mask that was lying on the deck in the dark, and decided he would offer the girl two hundred and fifteen escudos for it.

And he sat and waited, swaying and restless, for the second whistle and the second stop.

2

The house was in darkness. He went in through the screendoor and let it swing shut gently behind him. The veranda smelled dead and everything was silent apart from the rasping of crickets outside in the yard.

He went to sit in the large chair under the buffalo head and, after a while, closed his eyes. Everything was familiar again: the sweet smell of mango blossoms and frangipani, the slightly mouldy smell of the house, the crickets – even the crickets' racket was different to that in Caipemba. In his imagination he could again hear the regular thudding of the boat's engine and the mbira, and it felt as if the chair swayed slightly beneath him.

He was tired.

Gonçalo and the girl would probably have passed the hippo pool by now. It would take at least an hour to her camp; possibly a little more than an hour. They would be at the camp at ten o'clock at the earliest.

He could again see the lantern disappearing through the trees. Gonçalo initially walked behind and the light fell on her red dress and on her calves, and then Gonçalo went past her and he could only see her silhouette as they disappeared behind the banana trees.

One of the screendoors on the veranda closed with a gentle bump. Delport wanted to get up and see who it was, but he couldn't get that far; he was tired out and wanted to sit. He opened his eyes and looked towards the front door, listened, but just at that moment a cricket began its racket in the roof and he could not hear anything any more.

The screendoor disappeared and he again saw the girl walking away down the path in the dark, her shadow a pendulum in front of her in the light of Gonçalo's swinging lantern. That reminded him of the handkerchief and he took it out of his shirt pocket and inhaled its scent.

That did more for him than all the pictures on Rodrigues's wall.

You only live once, he thought, although one of Rodrigues's books speculated otherwise. One morning on the way to Caipemba he had taken the book from Rodrigues's shelf, and read on the first page – you only live twice – your own life and the life you dream of. The second half of the sentence was underlined in pencil.

Grant me these few pictures, Rodrigues had said. If the real thing continually evades you…

But Rodrigues chose the pictures above the real thing. The pictures were always available, would never leave him in the lurch, would not die suddenly on a good day in November. Rodrigues preferred the pictures because he no longer had any faith in the real thing. He was scared of the real thing.

Unlike João. He stood up, without thinking, poured a whisky in the dark and went to fetch some water in the fridge and thought: better like João, then.

He had stood in the light of a lantern, waiting on the bank when they drew up to the second stop. It was the same João as always – the João of the previous week and the previous year: a middle-aged man wearing shorts and gaiters; shorts, that like his bush jacket and his white pith helmet and his false teeth and gaiters, were at least three sizes too big. Only his boots almost fitted.

He stood dead still until the gangplank touched the ground. Only then did he take out his wire-rimmed glasses, put them on and approach. Without his glasses he could barely see ten paces in front of him, but he only put his glasses on when he found himself in unknown terrain. In his yard and in his house they were unnecessary.

"Delport!" he called out as the first natives started coming down the gangplank. "Are you there?"

Delport went down and greeted him.

Behind the gazebo with its roof made of palm fronds he could see João's Harley Davidson, at the edge of the lantern's light, the sidecar glittering in the shadows. João saw him looking at the motorcycle and said: "Ride with me. I'm just getting my salt."

"I can't," said Delport, but João was already at the pier, busy talking to Rodrigues. A native came down the gangplank, bent double under the weight of a large sack of salt and carried it past Delport and let it fall into the motorcycle's sidecar. João regularly got salt from Caipemba for the preparation of animal hides. He could not order more than one sack at a time because the motorcycle was his only means of transport.

"Max is coming the rest of the way with me," he heard João tell Rodrigues. "Don't wait for him."

"I can't." Delport went over to João. "I can't ride with you. There is someone I must..." Suddenly he did not know what to say, because at that moment the girl appeared at the railings.

"You must what?" João wanted to know.

Delport didn't answer.

"I want to talk to you, *amigo*." João took him by the arm and led him to the gazebo.

"What is it?"

João took his glasses off and pondered for a moment and pushed them back over his ears. "I don't know," he said. "I wanted to..." He hesitated a moment; then asked: "Is everything okay?"

"What do you mean?"

"Nothing, just asking."

Delport could only stand and stare at him. He didn't know what to say.

"Are you coming?" Rodrigues called from the boat.

"Go." João was suddenly embarrassed. "Go on," he said. "We can talk later." And he turned away, got on to his motorbike and kicked it into life.

Delport went back on to the boat.

They pulled the gangplank up after him and he could still hear the motorcycle idling, but he did not look back – not until the boat was some distance away from the bank. And only then did João put the motorbike in gear and pull away from the small circle of the lantern's light.

Outside, a door slammed shut again. Delport finished his whisky and stood up. He could see the veranda through the screendoor and there was no one there. He went to the child's room. The child was not in his bed. The rooms of both Ann and

33

the child's opened on to the veranda and the doors were close to each other, the child's at the edge of the veranda and Ann's just next to the corner. Delport looked into Ann's room. After a while he could make out the pale mosquito net and a little later he saw the child standing, next to the bed, dead still. The child stood looking at the mosquito net. Delport could not decide if the child was aware of him, and he waited, and the child did nothing, just stood unmoving, looking down at the bed next to him, as if waiting, as if listening to something Delport could not hear.

The only sound was that of the crickets. A monotonous choir, with the intermittent croak of a frog somewhere in the darkness.

But then, as he listened, as he waited for the child to do something, there was another sound.

Somewhere in the yard there were footsteps. Delport turned his head and looked outside. But there was no movement. He went down the steps and stood beneath the mango trees and when he stood still he could hear the footsteps getting closer, from the direction of the river. And when he turned around he sensed a presence somewhere nearby – recognised the pith helmet, and the baggy bush jacket. It was João Albasini.

Delport took a deep breath and said nothing. It was João who spoke first. He nudged his pith helmet a little further back on his head and came right up to Delport and asked: "How are you, *amigo*?"

"I didn't hear your motorbike coming."

"I got here before you arrived. I left the bike back at the servants' quarters; I was afraid of waking you people up."

There was a fleeting moment of lightning and in that moment Delport noticed the path and João's glasses.

"Is she here?" João asked.

"Who?"

"The girl."

"No," said Delport and suddenly understood. And he smiled.

"Do you know her?" João wanted to know.

"I met her this afternoon for the first time."

Albasini took off his glasses and put them in his pocket and said: "I don't like her."

"So you know her then?"

"No."

Delport could see him better now. João stood looking at the house and Delport was sure he could not see the house.

"What did you want to talk to me about tonight?"

"You're scared," said João. "Why?"

Delport just shook his head.

"When I walked up just now, you were scared."

"That's not what you wanted to talk about."

João was still looking in the direction of the house. And Delport turned round to make sure no one was there, and at the same time the lightning was somewhere again, more brilliant than the previous time, and he could fleetingly see the bougainvillea's purple flowers under the eaves and against the water tank, and alongside the water tank stood the child in his pyjama pants.

João was on edge. He was like an animal that could smell something on the air. But he tried to hide it.

"Is something bothering you, João?" Delport asked.

And João shook his head and said: "No. Why?"

"You wanted to talk to me."

"Not about anything in particular," he said. "I haven't seen you in quite a while."

Delport knew that was not the truth.

"Walk with me to my bike."

"Why?"

"We must talk."

"Rather come inside then."

"No." João shook his head. "It's going to rain soon."

That, too, was a lie. Because the rain was still some way off and João put his glasses on and they started walking, around the house, across the back yard. The lightning flashed twice, three times in short succession, and in the light Delport could see the child's roadways in the soft sand – twisting roads that criss-crossed and forked and disappeared in the darkness.

They walked swayingly side by side, João's strides long and like a lion's, wiry. There was nothing to say.

This moment always came for Delport, even with the two or three people whom he knew well: the moment at which he realised the conversation was over, even though there was lots left to talk about.

He wanted to talk to Albasini about the girl, but he didn't know how. Because in the end there was nothing he could tell – apart from the mask. Despite that, he wanted to talk about her.

But they were at the motorbike before he could find the right words. João hesitated for a moment, as if he too wanted to get something off his chest, but he suddenly grabbed on to the handlebars and swung a long leg over the saddle and straightened his glasses.

"What did you want to talk about?"

"Since last week there's been a camp up at Dois creek."

"I know," Delport said.

"That woman who was on the boat tonight –"

"I know."

"Did they come by here?"

Delport shook his head.

"You must do something about it."

"Yeah."

"I was wondering if you knew." Albasini pushed down on the kick-starter, fed the engine. *"Boa noite."**

"Is that all you came to tell me?"

"I was just wondering how things were going. *Boa noite.*" He turned the motorcycle, then shouted over his shoulder for the third time *"Boa noite!"* and rode off.

Delport didn't wait. He walked back through the yard and listened to the drone of the motorcycle dissipate in the night.

Closer to the house he stood still. He was sure he had heard a door close somewhere. He stood dead still and waited and after a while he could make out Fernando's large shape. The native was coming towards him from the side, obviously unaware of his presence, and only stopped when Delport spoke.

"Where've you come from?" he asked.

Fernando stood for a moment without answering. "I'm being finished," he said eventually.

"You weren't in the kitchen."

---

* Boa noite – Good night

"I went to put the Dona's glass of water."

"You must get things done earlier, man," Delport said, and his voice betrayed him. "This lazing about around the house until so late at night is unnecessary."

The native did not respond – just stood a while staring quietly at Delport and then walked away, without saying goodnight.

Delport went into the house.

He hesitated for a moment on the back veranda, then went into his room and stood in front of the window. An insect was fluttering against the ceiling. He could hear the soft, searching sound of the wings. The room smelled mouldy and the smell was familiar and calming.

He waited for the lightning again, his eyes on the tank where the child had been standing earlier. When the lightning struck, a minute or two later, he saw the child: he was still standing in the same place, but now facing in the opposite direction.

And he leant out of the window and called softly in the darkness. Twice, three times. But there was no answer.

When the lightning struck again, the child was no longer there.

He went to lie on the bed, saw the girl walking ahead of him down the gangplank, her leather bag swinging against her body. He was a little way behind her and Gonçalo had already gone ahead of them, standing waiting on the bamboo pier, the two large provision sacks on either side of him.

"*Adeus!*" Rodrigues called from behind them, his face framed by tendrils of blue smoke. "Have a good evening!"

They waved over their shoulders and walked to the end of the pier before coming to a stop. The gangplank had already been raised and the boat had started moving, slowly swung its keel into the stream, drifted off. They stood next to each other and watched the boat ploughing ahead, with Rodrigues alone on the top deck, until his form and the outline of the boat melded with the darkness and only a splash of light from the bottom deck drifted eerily in the darkness.

It was only then that they became aware of each other's presence. The chugging of the boat was just a vague sound behind the choir of frogs and crickets and the susurration of reeds in the river.

"I'll walk with you," he said. "Gonçalo will bring a lantern just now."

"It's not necessary," she said.

"You can't go by yourself."

"I'll be okay."

"It's a long way," he said. "I'll go with."

"You've already done enough for me today, *senhor*." She sounded adamant. "I'm not scared of the dark. If you could only lend me a lantern. I'll bring it back."

"I'll worry about you," he said. "The world is rough around here. Besides, you don't know the way."

"I do," she said. "I've come here along the path before." He looked up at the dark blot of her face.

"When?"

She hesitated for a moment. Or was it longer than only a moment? Then she said: "I was bored."

The Mahala's light disappeared and Delport looked in the direction of his house. There was still no sign of Gonçalo. "We can go and wait up there," he said. "I'll walk in front. I know the way."

"If you can just lend me a lantern."

"I'll send Gonçalo with you. He's very reliable."

She did not answer.

Somewhere in the darkness, not very far away from them, there was a brief whistle. And then another. She must also have heard it, because she stood still.

"It's a reedbuck," he said.

"Do they whistle like that?"

"They whistle just like people do."

She followed him up the steep incline to where it flattened out and the path forked.

She stood close to him and her breath was racing somewhat from the climb.

"Will it be okay for Gonçalo to go with you?"

"If it is that important to you," she said and nodded. "But I would have been okay by myself."

"Yes, perhaps. And perhaps not."

"I was actually looking forward to it. To walking by myself."

The small yellow circle of the lantern suddenly appeared in the distance between the trees and bobbed closer.

"*Senhora*," Delport said, "that mask…"

From her voice he could hear her smile as she asked: "You must like it a lot?"

"I'll give you two hundred and fifteen escudos. That's all I've got on me." He didn't want to look at her, his eyes were fixed on the approaching lantern.

"I can't sell it to you," she said.

Gonçalo was jogging. He was one of the few blacks on the reserve who sometimes got it into his head to get his arse moving.

"Is everyone asleep already?" Delport asked when Gonçalo came to a stop five paces away from them.

"The house is dark, *amo*."

"Will you walk with the Dona? Her camp is an hour's walk from here."

Gonçalo nodded.

"Watch your step. And come and let me know when you get back. I won't be able to sleep."

"*Obrigado*," the girl said, and when he looked at her, he saw her holding something out to him. It was the mask.

"Think over it for a while first," he said. "You don't have to decide immediately. I'm sure I'll see you again."

"I've made up my mind."

He did not know what he should do. His hand was already slightly raised to take it from her, but the fact that she had given in, suddenly made him feel guilty. Eventually he took it from her and put his hand in his pocket to take out his wallet.

"It's for the help," she said.

"I'll give you two hundred and fifteen escudos."

But she shook her head, turned away and began walking off. And Gonçalo followed on behind her.

"*Senhora!*" Delport called. "Hold on…"

They carried on walking, her and the native, and after a while Gonçalo went past her. And Delport stood and watched them disappear behind the sweet mango trees.

He woke up from the noise.

Only when he heard it for a second time did he realise that it was Ann who was screaming. But he didn't get up immediately; he hoped she would go back to sleep again. Her bedroom window was diagonally across on the back veranda, ten paces away from his door, and he could hear her murmuring softly and suddenly there was a third scream.

He was still dressed and he got up and went to her room. He seldom went into her room; only at night when she became restless.

The mosquito net was half open and he lifted it up and sat on the edge of the bed and looked at her. She was lying on her back and it was as if she was sliding back into sleep, but her mouth was slightly open and her fingers clutched the bed frame.

There was just a sheet over her lower body and the buttons on her nightie were undone; he could see one of her breasts and the dark stain of her nipple. She let go of the bed frame and tried to lift herself up, then fell back again and turned on to her side, curled up, groaning, and began mumbling again.

"You must get some sleep, Ann," he said.

Through the open window he could see the child approaching across the back yard. The moon must have broken through the clouds somewhere, because the yard was brighter than before. The child came right up to the window and pressed his face against the glass, his hands hanging at his sides.

"Hold me," she whimpered, and Delport knew she was not talking to him.

She kicked her legs straight and screamed again, her hands under her arms as if she were embracing herself. He shook her by the shoulder and talked to her, softly, and felt how she relaxed a little.

"Don't leave," she said; this time he could hear her clearly.

"I won't," he said, even if the words had not been meant for him. He wanted to say something to placate her.

When he stood up the child was no longer at the window. He pulled the sheet over her, rearranged the mosquito net and left. Somewhere in the yard he could hear the child imitating the drone of a car, getting further away, until he could no longer be heard.

The lightning was no longer flashing and the moon was a pale circle behind the clouds. But while he was still looking at it, the circle darkened until there was nothing left of it. Suddenly it was so dark that he had to feel his way to the living room.

He did not want to admit it to himself, but João's visit was bothering him. João was keeping an eye on the house as if there was something he was suspicious of, and there was something absentminded in everything he said and did: his thoughts were elsewhere. But he was scared of talking; he was hesitant to say what was going on in his head.

Perhaps he had expected the girl to be there. Perhaps he had wanted to spy on them. Why else did he park so far away from the house, wait for them at the river, and not come out immediately when they got off the boat?

Where exactly was he when they got off? He must have hidden away somewhere.

Delport went to sit under the buffalo head. The mask was next to the chair on the floor and he picked it up and unwrapped it, ran his fingers over it.

João had never been inquisitive, he thought; he had never gone to so much trouble to find out something about someone else. He had always forged his own path, never allowed himself to be dragged into anything, looked after his animals, sold his hides, unconcerned with the trials and tribulations of others.

Delport suddenly believed it beyond any doubt: João knows the girl; but something prevented him from showing it.

The yard was smouldering outside, out of sight; the air was heavy and sweet and empty of sound – even the frogs were quiet. The lonely song of a mosquito was all that remained. It was as if the stifling air and the darkness smothered everything and isolated it in the silence.

He saw Ann clutch at the bed frame in pain. Her hair was ragged with sweat and the candle's flame next to her bed was motionless and white. When she screamed the door opened and the woman came in and asked if she was still bleeding. Ann nodded and the woman said that's good – the more she bleeds, the better. The blood must flush her clean. And when the woman left, he got up and went to sit next to the bed and held her hand. She said: "Don't go, Max." He shook his head and said nothing.

The room smelled of Dettol and in the corner on the white table there were wads of blood-stained cottonwool and a pair of scissors and a syringe and a wash basin with the light-red water in which the woman had washed her hands.

"He won't come back, will he?" she asked and he knew what she meant and said no, he's gone for good. He is in the past.

"Ritter," she said and he let go of her hand and went to sit and said Ritter is far away, she is scared for nothing – he is with her and he will help her.

He wanted to help her. He loved her. That's why he lied and denied and humiliated himself to help her and look after her. He would not leave her in the lurch. That summer had seen enough betrayal.

Ritter was locked away and powerless and it was possible to be brave again.

But she was bleeding more than seemed safe to him and her face was paler than the whitewashed wall; he could not help but be scared – the doubt invaded him and became a sort of self-reproach and by daybreak bravery was not a consideration any longer. Ritter wanted an eye for an eye, even though he was locked up.

The woman did not come again. At sunrise someone peered through the window, hands hanging at his sides, and Delport snuffed the candle out, tucked the blankets underneath her and carried her out of the house with the cursing of Ritter's name reverberating like a bell in his hollow chest.

They were burning sugarcane on the hills above Tongaat and the sun rose blood-red through the banks of smoke. But just that once Ritter had drawn the short straw.

Delport took the Birth mask below the buffalo head off its nail and hung up Ritter in its place. The mbira was tied to the same nail with sisal string and while he fumbled in the dark to hang the mask, he touched one of its keys and heard the thin sound hesitating in the room for a long while afterwards.

Only when it was quiet again did he then go to his room.

He got undressed and threw his pyjama pants over his shoulder. In the bathroom he tipped a bucket of water into the shower drum and stepped under the lukewarm drops and washed himself. He then pulled his pyjama pants on to his wet body.

Ann seemed to be asleep.

He wanted to go looking for him. Somewhere among the day's groceries was a blue clockwork car. But that would have to wait until the following day, because to call him would be hopeless; he wouldn't answer – and to look for him in the dark, would be just as fruitless. He had, despite repeated threats and sweet-talking, often wandered off from the homestead overnight.

In his room, he put the girl's handkerchief away in his wardrobe and went to lie on the bed, without thinking about sleep. Drowsiness seldom triumphed over the heat until well past midnight.

Sometimes, at this time of night, there was music on the radio and he looked for a station. During the day the green reception indicator would flicker fruitlessly when it was switched on; crackling and almost inaudible voices were all that the speaker could conjure up.

There was only one station that could be heard free of any interference – to the extreme left of the dial. He always found it easily, because it was the only place where the green eye stopped flickering. But the station was not on air – all that could be heard was a short signature tune that was played over and over again: a tune with eleven notes, played on a single mbira; four bars, of which the first three were the same, three notes each, and the fourth two notes. It was much like the call of a lourie, just as monotonous, just as sombre and lonely.

Delport turned the dial back and forth, from left to right and back, again to the right and back, searching. There were voices, almost inaudibly vague, and snippets of music now and again, interspersed with irritating noises, as if a veld fire was raging in the depths of the speaker.

He must have fallen asleep, because he was standing and looking again at the small hole in the screen on the door to Ann's room. In his dream he knew he was sleeping; he knew he was dreaming that he was standing and watching, trapped by the bullet-shaped hole – the blackened points of the wire gauze all similarly bent towards the inside: a hundred almost invisible fingers pointing directly at her. He stood there for a long time, then turned around and went out into the quiet yard and left footprints on the damp ground, over the child's meandering roads, and followed a road that suddenly came to an end – just any old place – where the child lay and slept, the grader plank still in his hand.

He must have fallen asleep, because when he became aware of the radio again, it was raining outside. There was wind in the trees and the curtains were flapping over his face. He did not close the window immediately; the bed was already wet. He took a deep breath and felt the warm rain wash over him and listened to the rain on the roof and to the mbira's sombre tune next to him in the dark.

It was like that every summer: the first rains came during the night, soon after spring, unexpected. There would be lightning at night for weeks on end; during the day the flies would sit lazily on the gauze, there would be more mosquitoes, centipedes would begin moving around, the green pigeons would call until sunset, with the air becoming heavy and hard like steam. But the rain would stay away – long enough to set your mind at ease and allow you to forget the warning signs. And then one night it would come, without any further warning, softly over the plains, together with the wind.

João was right. He had forecast rain.

He had a way of foreseeing things. That was a little ironic. He worried little about the future, even less than about the past. The present was enough for him.

Delport closed the window and went to stand in front of the screendoor. He could not see the rain but it was enough to smell it and listen to it.

Somewhere in the house a window was slamming, open and shut, in the wind, and he went from room to room, closing the windows, fetched tin cans and put them under the leaks in the roof.

The child was lying across his bed, on his back and slept with an open mouth.

He went to stand over the child and took the matches from beside the lamp and struck one: his eyelids were paler than the rest of his face, and thin – almost transparent; his ears were two white carnations against the side of his head; his mouth was soft and defenceless as only a child's could be; his hands were open and relaxed.

Only when he slept could Delport get so close to him. He stood and looked at him until the flame burnt his fingers, then ran his fingers through the child's hair in the dark, quick and guileless. The child turned over on to his stomach and continued sleeping, his head turned, his arms underneath him, and one leg pulled up slightly as if he was protecting something.

He remembered the clockwork car and went to fetch it and put it next to the bed, in a place where the child would see it when he woke up.

And still it rained, harder than a few minutes before. There was no lightning any longer, but now and again, in the distance and over the rustle of the rain on the roof, he could hear the weather rolling away through the night.

On the front veranda, Delport suddenly stopped in his tracks. He wanted to look at his watch, but it was too dark. In the child's room, where there was no wind, he lit another match and held it to his wrist.

It was a quarter to twelve and Gonçalo was not back yet!

They had left at nine o'clock. The camp was near the confluence of Dois creek and CCG's irrigation overflow channel – an hour on foot. He should have been back by eleven o'clock. He would have jogged most of the way back, because it was late and he would have wanted to get back before the rain. Even if the rain had overtaken him, he would not have sought shelter by the side of the path. Gonçalo was familiar with these first rains; he would have known that it did not let up before dawn. Besides, no native ever hid from the rain; for them to be wet by the rain meant to receive the blessings of Umlenzengamunye.

Delport got dressed and went out in the darkened yard in the rain, between the trees, through to the servants' quarters. The stream was quiet, there was still no audible flow – but the ground was saturated and here and there he was ankle-deep in the water.

It was good to hear it, after all those months of sun: the tap-tapping of drops on his hat and on the leaves, the trees' wet rustling in the dark wind. He kept to the path, through the banana trees, his shoes slip-sliding in the mud patches, his trousers damp and cold around his calves, arriving near the stream where the grass opened out, revealing the nakedness of the clearing around the servants' quarters.

Gonçalo's hut was the nearest and he bent at the door, with the cold drops pricking his cheeks, and called out. He could feel large drops from the edge of the roof falling on to his neck and he listened to see if anyone answered, but all he could hear was the rain and the gurgling stream.

He called out again and again to Gonçalo and eventually the door opened, just a crack, but he could not see anybody. "Gonçalo?"

"He's not back yet," someone said. It was a child's voice.

Delport went to Kiya's hut and hammered at the door. "Are you there, Kiya?" There was life inside – a soft thump against the reed wall. "Get dressed!" he said when the door opened. "Hurry up."

He went to wait to one side and after a while Kiya came out from between the huts in a jacket, his service rifle in an oilskin over his shoulder. "I'm ready, *amo*," he said.

They walked one after the other, Delport in front.

Only after they were a kilometre away did Kiya say: "I didn't hear anything."

He was seldom called out at night. It only happened when shots were heard and they had to go searching for poachers.

"I also didn't hear anything." Delport's pace was fast, but he was used to it and still far from tired.

Kiya weighed up the matter for a long while. "Where are we going then, *amo*?" he asked at last.

Delport told him. And the reason, when he mentioned it aloud, suddenly struck him as somewhat unusual. Gonçalo was not back yet; he was late – an hour late. But in the bush no one kept track of time. There was only day and night; there were no hours. Nothing happened too early and what happened too late, still always happened in time.

But this time it was different. Delport knew it without questioning himself. At night no one took an unnecessary detour, especially not if it was raining and somewhere a wife was lying waiting under a warm blanket. Although Gonçalo did not talk back, he had nevertheless not been eager to tackle the journey so late at night.

They went past the hippo pool and the water was lying higher than usual. The bulrushes and sedges on the island in the middle of the pool, that usually stood high and dry, were now half under water.

At times the sky opened a little and outlined clumps of trees against the line of the horizon. Then the rain floated down in small, barely audible droplets. But not long afterwards the darkness would settle again and the rain would fall more determinedly, an invisible wall of water without any wind or lightning.

Once they were past the hippo pool, Kiya overtook Delport and walked in front. He and Delport knew the terrain equally well, but the dark and the rain led the white man to lose direction sometimes and Kiya could see better in the dark.

They never spoke when they were out in the bush. Words were largely superfluous. They spent almost every day together in the bush and understood each other well. That night, too, almost nothing was said; for Delport it was enough to see Kiya's silhouette in front of him with the rifle across his neck.

Delport constantly expected to hear someone coming towards them, to see Gonçalo appearing out of the darkness, his lantern a hazy circle of light in the rain. But the further they went, the less he thought about that. The only sign of life was a hyena that trotted away from them, hunched over, in the path, an owl that flapped up between wet leaves, and a chameleon, clutching on to a piece of grass, that opened its yellow mouth in the lantern's light as Delport went past.

It reminded him of the mask and he remembered Ritter, but they were vague thoughts that never completely took root. Everything was reduced to staring blindly into the dark rain and a persistent drudging on the narrow path into the wet night. Even thoughts of the girl were fleeting. Perhaps he did not want to be thinking about her.

Where the path went through the creek over large stepping stones, Kiya stopped. The water flowed darkly past, the stones were covered. Neither of them offered an opinion. They stood and looked at the stream and after a while Kiya went into the rushing water, but the flow was too strong and he was barely up to his knees in the water when he turned round and struggled back, step by step.

They sought out a broad tree and went to sit and wait. The rain abated slightly and, in the south, the sky was beginning to open. With the rain petering out, the cold made an entrance.

Delport was more tired than he had realised; he sat with his back against the tree trunk and fell asleep against his will.

Perhaps it was in his sleep or perhaps he was awake now and again, but he asked himself over and over again why he was in such a hurry to follow in Gonçalo's tracks.

A lot had happened to him since the sun had gone down. The previous afternoon he had not yet made the acquaintance of Mália Domingo. He had been on his way home like on all the previous occasions. He was tired and he wanted to get home and pour himself a whisky and listen to the night and the silence.

And the girl had jumped down from the veranda of a shop and headed for him, between the flies and the fruit baskets, and spoke to him. That was the beginning of everything. And he could not know that it would send him into the rain before daybreak in search of a lost Gonçalo. That brought him back to the cold and godforsaken moment where he and Kiya sat in the dark waiting for the Dois creek to subside.

It was near dawn when the native woke him up. "We can get through, *amo*," he said.

Delport stood up and his body was sore and stiff when they went up to the water and strode in. They struggled slowly but surely through the stream and the water came up to their hips. But they could see where they were going and it was not too difficult.

The light was grey on the trees and when they went past the second hippo pool they could already see the glittering droplets on the grass stalks, and there were lilac-breasted rollers in the trees.

There was still no sign of Gonçalo.

The camp couldn't be much further now; another quarter of an hour's walk at the most. Something was out of place and Delport expected that he would make Gonçalo pay for the trouble he had caused. The order to him had been clear and nothing was reason enough to disobey that order.

The second time that Kiya came to a stop was on a sharp turn in the path. Delport came up behind him and then turned out of the path and stopped.

There was a patch of burnt grass, a few yards wide. It was obvious that the rain had put a stop to the fire. Gonçalo's lantern was lying by the side of the path, at the edge of the patch of blackened grass tufts. The glass was black from smoke and partially covered with ashes, but it was in one piece.

And Gonçalo was also there. He was lying in the path, on his stomach, his hands by his sides, like someone asleep. He was lying perfectly comfortably.

Kiya stood to one side and took the rifle from around his neck and rested the butt on the ground. Delport walked up to Gonçalo and slowly rolled him over and there appeared to be nothing wrong with him. But he was already stiff and above his right eye there was a small round bullet hole.

3

That first summer next to the river it had rained almost every day, but it had provided no relief at all from the heat. By seven in the morning the earth was already sweltering under a brooding, malicious sun and by eleven one's ears were painful from the cicadas. In the afternoons, the air contracted and, by four, everything was purple and grey and the sweat streamed from one's body. At five, the lightning would draw blue streaks over the plains and the rain would break from the sky and pour down in heavy grey sheets.

But nothing mattered. The heat was good enough, and the rain was good, and the loneliness was no burden; even the mosquitoes and the leaking house and the puffadders in the drinking water were bearable. Because Ann was with him and Ritter was just a vague memory. Ann laughed and she did not mind.

She was still sick, sometimes; she was thin and there were dark rings under her eyes and she slept most of the time. But in the afternoons she would be waiting for him and they would walk to the river and in the evening after supper, feed geckos on the windowsill in the lounge.

That first month had gone by and that was consolation enough. That month of flight and begging and the eventual single room in Beira's harbour with him coming back night after night with no hope of a way out – at least that was something of the past.

He never spoke about himself. At night when he lay down and listened to whether he could hear footsteps in the yard outside or not, at night when he lay down and wondered where Ritter was looking for him, he pretended to be asleep. He even pretended to snore when he knew she was awake. He had paid a steep price for what he had and he did not want to lose it.

He never allowed her to go to Caipemba alone. He made sure that he stayed close to her. He was alert and on his toes. His eyes were open. As a child he had heard the blacks say: watch out if you see an earthworm crawling on the ground; tread carefully if you see a chameleon or lizard staring straight at you, or a hammerhead flying out of your way; be warned if a hyena spends the day stalking or following you, or if an owl calls from your roof at night. They are all signs. Delport did not believe in such things, but he was ready, every day, every night, even in the unlikeliest of places, he was ready to see a door swinging open suddenly, to see a bush moving, a crowd of pedestrians making way – to see that tall lissom man appear out of the sun, at ease, as always, relaxed, and smiling, that man with the thick golden hair and the morbid mouth, his right hand in the pocket of his bush jacket, his eyes cold and sympathetic and paternal and small under the solid eye sockets.

He had loved him, once. He had loved Ritter as a man loved his father. Ritter was so much better than he was. He knew and understood everything; he had advice for everything. He could talk about the world as he could about the palm of his hand. He saw a chance for everything and nothing was too difficult for him. He always, always won.

Only the once had he misjudged: that night at Ballito. Everyone involved in the matter had agreed that he had misjudged, although no one could know for sure. They merely guessed, because Ritter did not want to explain anything to anyone. And this one crucial, small lapse had changed everything.

Delport was thinking of that night at Ballito while sitting on his haunches and looking at Gonçalo. Because that was the first time since that night that he had seen a corpse again. And when he had let the stiff cadaver roll over on to its face again, it was like back then, once again. Only, the first time the corpse had still been warm.

They put the body in the shade and Kiya remained behind. He went on by himself.

He did not walk quickly. He was tired and Gonçalo's death had caught him unawares and had left him feeling even more tired. He walked and thought: whatever happened, it was unnecessary; it was completely unnecessary and Gonçalo did not deserve it.

There was something else as well: a vague concern about the girl. He did not want to think about that, but something was constantly telling him that Gonçalo was not alone when he had been shot. He was scared of getting to the camp; he was afraid he would not find her there and he did not want to consider that possibility. The death of two, three was more than enough. He did not want to consider the possibility of a fourth.

Over the final kilometre, he rested twice.

He saw the truck first; a grey 1948 Chev. It was standing between a copse of acacia thorn trees and a mahogany tree and there was a tarpaulin over the back of the pick-up truck. The riverbank was not more than twenty paces from the truck's front wheels.

It was much too close, Delport thought, but the thought was not important at that moment. There was also no smoke – that was more to the point.

He turned off the path and headed through the short grass straight towards the camp, his shadow stretched out far behind him, and then he saw the canvas lean-to on the other side of the lorry. He kept on walking until he was five paces from the right rear wheel and then stood still and listened.

Everything was dead quiet.

It was only when the lilac-breasted roller stopped calling that he realised the bird was sitting in the mahogany tree. And for him that was the final proof that no one was in the camp.

He walked around the back of the lorry and went in under the lean-to. There were two deck chairs, a fold-up table laden with groceries, a paraffin tank with a primus on top, and a folded-up camp bed. There was a tin mug on the table, but the little coffee that remained in it was days old and full of dead ants. The primus was cold.

He walked around the front of the truck and looked at the number plate. It was from Beira. The window on the driver's side was rolled down and the front seat, wet from the rain. He walked round to the back again and tried to look into the back, but when he touched the tarpaulin, the girl inside asked:

"*Quem é?*" Delport took a step backwards.

"Roberto?" the girl queried.

"It's me."

"*Quem?*" she asked again.

"Delport."

She was quiet for a long time and he waited and nothing happened.

"I came to see if you were here," he said.

She moved about somewhere inside and then it was quiet again and when she eventually spoke, her voice was closer to him. "*Que horas são?*"* she asked.

"Half-six."

"*É cedo,*" she said sleepily. "I'm getting dressed."

He went to sit under the lean-to and waited for her. But she only emerged a quarter of an hour later – in a khaki shirt and a narrow cotton skirt. Her hair was not combed and her eyes were heavy with sleep, but she smiled.

"Did you get all the way here safely last night?" he asked and put his hat on the small table next to him.

She nodded.

"How far did Gonçalo come with you?"

"All the way here," she said. "He lit a lantern for me and waited until I was in the back of the truck."

Delport looked around again. His footprints were the only ones on the wet ground. The rain had wiped everything away.

The girl sat and rubbed her eyes and yawned behind a cupped hand. "You're wandering around early," she said.

"Are you here all by yourself?"

"Until the others get back."

"Aren't you scared?"

"No."

"Who's Roberto?"

She smiled. "My dad."

"Do you often go away hunting with him?"

"This is the third time."

"Do you have a weapon with you?"

"Yes. A revolver." She tried smiling again. "I can shoot well. Better than you."

---

* Que horas são? – What is the time?

  É cedo. – It is early.

"Gonçalo is dead," he said.

She did not immediately realise what he was saying. The smile disappeared from her face, but only a while later did shock appear in her eyes. "The black man?"

He nodded.

"Did he drown?"

"What makes you think he drowned?" Delport wanted to know.

"The creek was flowing terribly fast last night. Look," she said and pointed at the grass laid flat by flowing waters just ten paces from the lean-to. "I wondered if he would get through the creek."

"Didn't you hear any shots after he'd left here?"

"No," she said. "Was he shot?"

He could have imagined it, but it was as if the colour suddenly drained from her face.

"Are you sure you didn't hear anything?" he asked.

"It began raining," she said. "Just as we got here. Where did it happen?"

"A kilometre away from here."

A lilac-breasted roller now began its call a little further away and the sound was as clear as glass in the bright morning.

When he looked at her again, her eyes were fixed on him. "You suspect me," she said softly.

He shook his head.

"Then why are you cross-examining me?"

"I just wanted to find out what you know."

"Is that why you came here?"

"I wanted to come and make sure you were safe. And I wanted to come and give you the money for the mask."

She looked away. "You must leave. Please."

"You're not safe here," he said.

"I've got a revolver. I can shoot." Then she looked at him again. "You probably want to see it. Compare the bullets."

"I wanted to come and check that you were safe. That's all."

"I'll be fine. Just go."

"I'll send someone to come and stay here."

"And if something happens to him as well?" She shook her head and then pressed one hand against her temple and looked at the ground, and suddenly there was a strange expression on her face,

almost as if she was in pain. "We had been talking the whole
way..."

"Gonçalo?"

She did not answer.

"He was the best of his kind," he said, just to be able to say
something.

It was already hot again. The sun was only barely risen and
the ground was almost dry and Delport could feel himself
beginning to sweat.

"It would be better if you left," she said and looked up at him,
and suddenly he realised she was scared.

He sat for a moment longer and did not know what to think.
Then he stood up. "I'll send someone. My game warden, perhaps.
He's very reliable. Kiya. I'll send him with a tent."

She shook her head. "I don't want anyone here."

He was still wearing the same clothes as the day before and
the two hundred and fifteen escudos were still in his pocket. He
took the notes out and put them down on the table.

"I'll come back later and see how it's going. If something
happens, you can send Kiya to come and call me."

He looked at her and saw she was not listening to him: her
attention was drawn to something on the other side of the creek.
He looked in that direction, but could not see anything.

The lilac-breasted roller was quiet, but in the thorn trees below
the camp a troupe of babblers chattered.

"You must go," she said. "Please. I don't want any more
trouble."

They chopped down a pole with Kiya's hunting knife and tied
the corpse to it, carried it on their shoulders. And the whole way
back he and Kiya said nothing to each other. Delport was afraid
and he did not know why. He wanted to turn round and go back
to Mália Domingo. He did not know why.

Rodrigues Pereira often said it. When they played chess or sat in
the mesh-enclosed deck and had a drink. Africa is a godforsaken
place. And with that he meant more than the words would say.
Delport knew that because he remembered a conversation from
that very first night when he got to know Rodrigues.

Ann had slept on the way back from Caipemba; she had already been under the weather for days. And the captain was drunk and most sympathetic and he had gone to lay clean sheets on his bed specially and invited her to go and lie down there. He had pulled a bottle of brandy out from under his bed and they had gone to chat in the bridge. And Rodrigues had talked about all sorts of things. He had told Delport about Africa as one tells a new neighbour about your town.

Delport knew Africa a lot better than the captain, because he had grown up in Africa. But he did not say anything. He was glad to have the company and he listened to Rodrigues as if every word was news to him.

And he quickly realised: for Rodrigues, Africa is a jungle with a river. For Rodrigues, Africa is a trading post with mango trees and palm trees and flies and black faces and a handful of rudderless whites. For him, Africa was exile and loneliness and an endless silence. "Africa," he had said that night, "is a waiting room full of strangers at an unknown station. And everyone's waiting and everyone's longing for home and the bloody train won't come."

Every time after that when Rodrigues spoke of the godforsaken place, Delport knew why he called it that. And Rodrigues was right. He was talking about himself and about the Mahala and of the view from his small porthole, and called that Africa and did not know that it also had many other names.

That afternoon on his bicycle on the way to João Albasini with the sun in the spokes and the sweat streaming from his body, Delport knew that the waiting would never come to an end. His fear had another name, but it was the same as Rodrigues's.

He rode in the right-hand track. The grass on the hump in the middle of the road had been pressed flat and in places there were black stripes in the dry bluegrass stalks – João's Harley Davidson was leaking oil.

The sun fell in patches over the two sandy tracks, between the thickets of trees that grew on both sides of the road. Here and there in the shadows there were still puddles of water from the previous night's rain, but he could not turn to avoid them and every time he had to lift his feet to avoid the splattering mud.

He thought about himself and about the world, and the world was a musty house with green gauze over the windows, antelope heads and geckos against the walls, pawpaw trees in the backyard; a house with spiders and green fungus; a house with a cricket in the roof and the smell of frangipani in every little room; a house that you slept in and kept watch on Fernando and thought and never spoke and waited for tomorrow while you tried to remember yesterday. The world is an isolated place, he had thought, and smiled and thought; a godforsaken place.

He had remembered so many thousand nights filled with the rasping of crickets; between twilight at dusk and twilight at dawn the singing of so many thousand mosquitoes, and drums pulsating almost inaudibly far away in the darkness, and a little green light flickering over foreign languages and *fados* from an unknown country. The suns and sins of so many thousand days had burnt into his body, while he waited and was afraid and sometimes braver – waited on a door that would open, a shrub that would suddenly move and open in front of the face of a man whom he sometimes still wanted to love.

The house was hidden away between trees. It was part of the bush, part of the sun and the shadow. It was a mushroom that once, a long time ago, had stopped growing, and now stood green-white and languished in the damp shade.

The house was a square beneath a flat roof without gutters or drainpipes. Front and back there was a veranda with wire gauze from floor to ceiling. There was no yard – just a bare patch with sickly lemon trees standing docile and budding.

In the backyard, a group of yellow-brown children were playing with mud and took turns to cough asthmatically. They did not see Delport arriving.

He stood his bike against the wire gauze and knocked. He could hear one of the women talking in the rear of the house, but no one came to open the door. He knocked again and a child began crying where the others were playing, but the house was quiet. Then he walked around to the back.

The woman was sitting on a chair next to the back door, in a circle of shade, a child on her lap busy breast-feeding from her.

The child was five or six years old and Delport could not remember if he had ever seen him before. He could also not decide whose of the two women's it was – he seldom saw them and both of them looked the same to him.

"Afternoon," he said. "Is João here?"

The child let go of her breast and looked at him, then sought out the nipple again and carried on drinking.

"He's at the camps," she said and made a lazy gesture with her head. She was barefoot and was wearing a long blue dress that would probably hang down to her ankles when she was standing. Her black curly hair was combed and plaited into braids which, here and there peered out from her red headscarf.

The other children now came nearer. There were six or seven.

Delport nodded and walked between the chicken coops and followed the path to where, a short distance further on, he could hear João shouting orders. The nearest enclosures were a hundred paces from the house, but scattered between them and the house were smaller wire cages filled with meerkats and monkeys and genets and mongooses.

The children followed in a line behind him, at a safe distance, and paid no attention to the woman who tried to call them back.

Later, one gathered together enough courage and ran past Delport, giving him a wide berth, to his father. "*Ubaba*," he called from far away, "Inkunzinyati is here!"

João was busy trying to get a zebra with a catch-pole, but the animal was wild and every time it burst through the raucous natives to go along the fence looking for an escape route. Its nostrils were flared and every time it got past them and ran into the mesh fence its eyes rolled back in their sockets to reveal the whites.

The animal's flanks were gleaming with sweat and its muscles were rippling under its shining, striped hide. It stormed straight at the blacks and sent them scattering and João was swearing, swinging at them with the catch-pole. "Why don't you stop it, you miserable buggers!" And the natives, terrified, set off after the animal and turned back towards the fence. They were scared of João; that was no secret; they were scared of him because he often did not hesitate to lay into them with a whip – and even though he was skinny, he was strong and still very quick for his sixty years. And there was the story that he was a sorcerer. That he had kept two of their women in his house and he was the father of at least eleven bastard children, did not make him all that popular, but at least raised him in their estimation.

The animal headed for the corner again and saw it was heading for a dead-end, then broke away, right past João, who sank low to the ground, like a leopard ready to pounce, and swung the catch-pole through the air and it settled on the zebra's neck. It was suddenly animal against animal. The zebra's front legs buckled under it and its nose ploughed into the dirt, and João almost fell over backwards and the noose pulled tight.

With the sudden throttling, the animal got to its feet again and was kicking its back legs and swung around so that its hindquarters were in João's direction. Then it reared into the air on its back legs and hit out with its front hooves. But João was like a nit. He clung on and let himself be dragged round with his heels ploughing two deep furrows through the damp ground. It was as if he was taunting the animal.

Delport stood unmoving and watched. It was as if the wrestling hypnotised him. He wanted it to continue like that, forever, the struggle, and at the same time he wanted to look away, because his heart was with the animal, but also not entirely – it was also with João's straining; he wanted to see the animal tamed and he wanted to see the animal break free and flee. He wanted to close his eyes and stop watching, but he could not – he could not even blink; he kept on watching.

There was froth around the zebra's mouth and the white stripes on its body had begun to darken under the sweat, until it came to a standstill with legs splayed, rocking and panic-stricken, and waited for the natives to approach it with ropes and tie up its hind legs. Then it stumbled and fell over and stayed there panting.

"He was a tough nut," João said later when he walked up smiling. "I'm almost inclined to just let him loose again."

Delport did not answer. He stood and watched how the natives struggled to load the animal on to a pallet and drag it away.

"He's been in the camp for a year already," João said, "I didn't think he would still be so wild. He'd been orphaned a long time."

"What are you going to do with him?" Delport asked at last.

"He's going to Beira. We caught six today. They're being put on the train tomorrow." The children began to approach inquisitively, but then scattered again when João suddenly turned round to face them. It was not necessary for him to say anything.

The women were still sitting in the shade when they got back to the yard.

"Bring another chair, Tanda," João ordered and the woman picked the child up off her lap and went into the house, coming out with a chair a short while later. She put the chair down next to the other one and disappeared again, and João indicated that Delport should sit down.

"How's it going?" he asked, his voice suddenly different, his eyes two anxious slits.

"So-so." Delport's thoughts were with the zebra. "And here, with you?" he asked and again saw the exhausted animal standing and waiting for the ropes – defeated and scared, but elated.

"So-so."

"When last did you have any poachers?"

João shook his head. "They stay away these days."

"You must keep your eyes open. Especially now."

João looked up. "Were you there this morning? At the camp?"

Delport had backed himself into a corner so that he had to shake his head. Then he asked: "Do you know how many of them there are?"

"Two, I believe. Three, with the woman."

They were sitting near the back door and Delport could hear the clink of teacups and from the black chimney a wisp of smoke now rose lazily.

"I'll keep an eye on them."

There were a few hens roaming freely, scratching in the dirt, and a little further away a turkey with a brood of chicks gobbled around. The child who had been drinking from Tanda, stood on the kitchen step picking his nose and kept an inquisitive eye on

Delport. His frizzy hair was so thin that one could clearly see his scalp. He was just as thin as his father, and also just as wiry.

Delport was looking for a way to tell João about Gonçalo, but he could not decide where he should begin. João was one of the few people he trusted, and even so he hesitated in dragging Mália Domingo into the matter; he wanted to avoid using her name.

A woman in a brown dress brought the coffee. That would almost certainly be Tombi. He stood up and greeted her, but João held him back when he went to take the tray from her. "She'll manage on her own," João said and his words made him think of the girl again.

They drank their coffee in silence and when the cups were empty João said they should go and sit on the front veranda. They walked through the kitchen (a dark little room with a coal stove, a crockery rack and a table with just one chair) and through the equally dark sitting room (four armchairs, a zebra skin on the floor and a carved wooden chest from Portugal). The veranda was cool. There were two canvas chairs, a few grass mats on the floor and three or four sets of antelope horns on the wall.

This was the first time in the nine years that Delport had known João that he had stepped into his kitchen and the second time that he had seen the inside of his sitting room. The single chair in the kitchen was indicative for him of the Albasinis' housekeeping. There were only two bedrooms, one on either side of the sitting room, and the natives said that João slept in the one and the two wives and eleven children all in the other one. He apparently sat alone at the table when they ate; the women and children seemingly sat on the floor, or the women on the floor and the children outside.

And while he had walked through the house, he had again – like that first time – thought of Rodrigues's cabin. The cabin was smaller than João's kitchen, but in those few cubic metres more worldly possessions were assembled than in all the four rooms of the Albasini household.

"There's something bothering you," João said after a while, and chewed on his loose false teeth.

Delport started from his daydreaming and smiled and nodded. "Gonçalo is dead."

"Your bearer?"

"He was shot through the head last night."

João said nothing.

"I found his body this morning, about eight kilometres from my place up on the path by Dois creek."

"Near the hunting camp?"

Delport hesitated and then nodded.

João took his pith helmet off and hung it on his knee. "He's the native who went with that woman," he said suddenly.

Delport realised he would not be able to hide anything from João and nodded again.

"But you didn't go to the camp?"

Delport nodded for a third time. "I did. Only the girl was there."

"And what did she say?"

"She didn't know anything. It wasn't her." Delport looked away, through the gauze, between the trees standing in front of the house and resonating with the sound of cicadas. He wondered why he was so eager to convince João of her innocence.

"Why did you come to my place last night?" he asked.

João did not answer – not immediately; only a little later when Delport looked at him did he sniff and rub a finger under his nose. "I wanted to come and chat."

"What about?"

Delport should have known better. He should have known João would not say anything. The question would only put him on the spot.

In all the years they had known each other, he had not once mentioned it; not about that nor about anything else relating to himself. He would talk about the weather, about his animals, sometimes about his wives, not about anything else. Nevertheless, now and again he betrayed himself. Sometimes he was restless, like on the previous evening, and then there was the night when he had come and woken Delport up with some or other incomprehensible story about the weather that had struck Ann and the child down dead. Delport had thought he was drunk, but he had not smelled of drink. And João would not leave before he had seen that Ann was alive and that the child was sleeping peacefully. After that, he had never again referred to that night and neither had Delport. Perhaps he knew nothing at all about it.

That is why it was strange when, in the afternoon, while they were outside and Delport already on his bike and ready to leave, he asked suddenly : "Who's staying with you?"

"No one," Delport said. "Why do you ask?"

And João had started walking off, very slowly, while Delport rode alongside him and twisted the front wheel to stay upright, from the yard until he reached the road. Then, a little further, a hundred paces from the house, João had stood still and looked back over his shoulder and then at Delport, and said: "There is someone at your place this afternoon."

Delport did not look surprised; he pretended that João had said something perfectly ordinary: it must be the girl – because he believed João. But he said: "I doubt there'll be anyone."

"The hunters perhaps."

"Could be."

"You must go back," João said, "but you must be careful." Then he looked away, and his eyes were tight slits again, those black eyes, small and hard from the African sun, suddenly smaller than usual. And he said: "He is standing in your sitting room and I can see what he sees." Delport said nothing, asked nothing, just waited for him to go on.

"Or perhaps," João said later, "he is standing in your bedroom. He is looking through a window with a green stain and he sees your water tank and he looks past the left of the water tank, under the outlet pipe. He sees your child playing underneath the pawpaw tree, and to the right of the pawpaws there's someone standing in the door of the storeroom."

Sometimes he was aware of it and sometimes not, on the way back: there were three sounds, all three equally continuous – the cicadas somewhere unseen in the sun, like light that has become sound; the swish of the bike's fat tyres in the track, clearer on the hard ground, duller in the sand; and in between, with monotonous regularity, the krr-click of the dry chain.

When he was aware of it, he listened to it, to its hypnotic quality, until the three distinct sounds became one. Then he tricked himself into believing that he could no longer hear anything, nothing apart from João's voice that said: he is standing in your sitting room and I can see what he sees...

It could be the girl. But for João it was a man. It could be the two hunters who had eventually showed up, or someone else who had come to have their hunting permit signed – but it was summer. They never came in the summer, only those looking for elephant, and they were few and far between.

It could be someone from CCG, but that was just as unlikely: over the many years there had never been anyone from the coffee farm who had come by.

He was tired and vaguely irritated. He blamed that on the puddles of rainwater that intermittently splashed up from under the front wheel and muddied his clothes, and on the humid air; the chatter of the bicycle chain irritated him. But he knew that these things were a distraction: he was furious about Gonçalo and about the camp at Dois creek and about the fact that, apparently, there was someone at home waiting to see him; someone he did not know.

Or perhaps – who could guess – perhaps it was Mália Domingo.

Delport smiled when he thought of that: the girl arriving out of the blue in his yard and looking for him. Would it make Ann wonder? Suddenly coming out of the bush, after nine years of nothing, a girl of nineteen who had come looking for him. Would it perhaps make Ann remember?

No, he thought. Through the krr and the click of the chain, no – beneath the swish of the tyres – nothing would bring her back again.

When the mbira had played outside their green window that afternoon in the town of João Belo, the girl had been ten; when they were on their way to Inhambane, while Ann was hungry and bleeding, the girl had been a child playing with dolls; when they had arrived that night in the deserted yard, had unlocked the house, checked the musty rooms and thought: we are going to be living here, we are going to make a life here, no one will ever find us here – that night Mália Domingo had been a child of ten.

How much had happened in between! So much, and so little.

In the north the air lay heavy and dark on the horizon. And

after a while the sun disappeared and the trees' shadows lengthened and lay expectantly waiting on the approaching night. This was the quietest time of the afternoon, with the first hadidas and lines of white egrets already heading silently to the river. The air was clammy and clingy and the rain would come with nightfall.

But Delport was not in a hurry. He rode slowly. Out of the corner of his eye he saw his jittery shadow flying over the bushes and grass and around tree trunks. Here and there, where there was too much water on the track, he got off and pushed the bicycle through the water, walking alongside on the hump between the two tracks that comprised the road. The final place where he had to climb off was four hundred metres from the house. He pushed the bike through the water and did not bother getting on again; he walked alongside the bike, one hand on the saddle, the other on the handlebars.

The house was a pale patch among the shadows. It was not completely dark yet, but in the servants' quarters the fires were already burning. The windows of the house were still dark and he could see the child standing near the kitchen, unmoving, as if watching someone among the banana trees.

As he got closer, the child heard him and looked towards him. "Hello," said Delport. "What do you see?" The child looked in the direction of the bananas again and shrugged his shoulders.

Delport stood and looked for himself, but there was nothing that attracted his attention. He pushed the bike to the kitchen and stood it against the wall, then looked at the banana trees again. There was still nothing, and the child had gone.

He could hear voices on the front veranda. It was Ann and Fernando talking, and it sounded to him as if they were arguing about something. He went quietly through the screendoor and stood on the back veranda and listened. But he could not make out what they were saying; just the once he imagined that he heard Ann saying the child's name. Then the door on the front veranda opened and shut.

Ann was busy watering some succulents in iron pots when he got to the veranda. She was just wearing her slip and she was barefoot. The native had gone. He looked towards the storeroom and the door was closed.

"Evening," he said.

She looked up. "Evening."

He walked up to her, placed his hand on her upper arm and kissed her on the forehead. She remained standing motionless and hard next to him. He could see that she was paler than usual. He wanted to pull her to him, but she resisted; he could feel how she pulled away from him.

"What's wrong?" he asked.

"It's so humid."

She watered the last of the three succulents.

"You should have put them outside," he said. "It's going to rain again tonight."

She looked at him. "Where were you the whole day?"

"I was home at twelve o'clock. You were in your room."

"I wasn't feeling well."

She put the watering can on the stand next to the succulents and he waited for her to say something more, but she said nothing. A bat dived out from under the eaves and disappeared squeaking into the twilight and the void.

"How are things here?" Delport asked.

She did not react for a moment, then made a gesture with her shoulder which could have meant anything.

"I was with Albasini," he said.

She went up to the gauze around the veranda and looked out over the yard, without reacting.

"Is everything here still…okay?"

She nodded. Then, a second later, looked at him, as if wondering why he asked that.

"Were you at home the whole day?" he asked.

"Yes. I wasn't feeling well."

He wondered if she knew about Gonçalo. The natives must have told her – or did they also perhaps know better? Perhaps they had not wanted to upset her. He would ask Fernando.

Her body was tired in the crinkled slip and on the one side of her face there were red wrinkles from sleep. He could scarcely believe the throat was the same one that he had discovered with his trembling, amazed lips a long time ago.

"When are you going to stop walking round in the house like that?" he asked.

"Like what?"

"You know what I'm talking about. That native was here with you on the veranda."

She looked up at him. "I'm dressed," she said and turned away. "Are you spying on me now?"

He did not want to say it. It was not what he planned on doing. In any case, it would not help to say it. Perhaps too much had already been said. But it was out before he could even think about it. "I wish I could take you away from here," he said.

And her answer was the same echo as before. "Where to?"

"Any other place in the world."

She turned away from the gauze. She was on her way to her room. He stopped her. But when she looked up and waited for him to explain, there was nothing more to be said. He let go of her arm and saw her open the screendoor and go into her room, up to her dressing table, sit on the only chair in the room in front of the mirror. He could see her back, and in the mirror her vague reflection, and deeper in the mirror his own, vaguer figure at the door.

When he spoke, it was as if he was speaking out of the mirror with her. "What good does it do staying here?" he heard himself asking.

"What good does it do to leave here?"

He could hear the child riding outside on his bike.

"Perhaps there is a place somewhere..."

She did not answer and he smelled the dust in the gauze in front of his face and the sweet flavour of mango blossoms.

"You're always sick here."

Somewhere in the room a cricket began chirping hesitatingly, softly. And their voices were even softer, more hesitant.

"I can't help that."

He nodded. "I know."

"It's better here."

He stood and looked at her, and she at his reflection. For a long time they said nothing. They listened to the cricket. Until he asked: "Did no one come round? Today?"

"No," she said. "Who were you expecting?"

The cricket stopped its noise.

"Nobody," he said.

He turned and went out into the yard. He walked to the storeroom and heard the child riding past on his bicycle.

The door was closed, but he could see Ann's footprint in front of the door – the only ones after the previous night's rain. She must have stood around at the door for a long time.

He went back to the house, to his room. The key to the storeroom was not on its nail. He looked towards the window and saw the water tank, and the pawpaw trees, and the storeroom door. But the door was left of the pawpaw trees, and not to the right as João had said.

If he were to stand in the sitting room and look, the pawpaws would be further left and the door would be visible to the right of them.

Ann had said there was no one.

He went to sit on his bed and in the semi-darkness began with searching fingers to pull grass seeds out of his damp socks. João must have imagined it. The one time that he got so far as to talk, he was wrong after all.

Or was he?

Ann had possibly been asleep. Or perhaps that was just when she had been at the storeroom.

He looked up, out of the window, and weighed up the possibility a moment longer.

He switched on the radio and immediately switched it off again, stood up, went out, to the kitchen. The kitchen was in darkness, but he could smell burning fat and hear Fernando at work in front of the stove.

"Fernando," he said. The noise stopped and a moment later the native answered him from nearby in the darkened room.

"*Amo...*"

"Was anybody here today?"

"No."

"Nobody?"

"Nobody."

He turned around to walk away, but stopped suddenly and spoke again. "Does the dona know about Gonçalo?"

"*Sim, amo,*" the native mumbled. "We told her."

He could feel it again, as with every time: the native's stiff manner of speaking, his straight back, his hesitancy – everything betrayed it: his concealed hostility.

Delport walked away.

He could not remember a green stain in the windowpane, but when he went into the room he saw it immediately. It was the middle pane just above the windowsill.

He looked to the left past the water tank, under the outlet pipe, right past the pawpaw trees. He could vaguely make out the storeroom door in the twilight.

But the stained pane was too low to look through. Delport bent lower. Even lower. He went down on to his knees – but that was a little too low.

The person must have been sitting.

He went to sit in the armchair. But that was also too low and too far to the left.

The room was just the same as always, the desolate order undisturbed. The Makonde figurine with the thin legs and the big fingers and the mbira hunched at an angle under the balled fist of its hump staring blindly into the twilight.

Delport raised himself up slightly and leant over to the right – and suddenly everything was neatly in the square of the green window pane: a part of the water tank, the place under the pawpaw trees where the child would have been playing, the door of the storeroom.

And while he was looking at it, he suddenly clicked.

It was incredibly simple, and it was inconceivable.

Behind him, against the wall, right behind his head, half a metre away from him, was the new mask.

4

That night they did not know what they should expect. So they said nothing to each other. Ann was, nevertheless, too sick to wonder about such things or to listen to his speculation. Rodrigues Pereira was there and he was a little drunk; he kept on talking and gave no one else a chance to say anything or, secretly, to wonder about the future.

He had tried to persuade them to first go past as far as Lotsumo, because it would be dark when they arrived at the third stop. "Lotsumo is not really a place," he explained, "but old Schwulst is still there and old Schwulst has a hotel – a hotel of sorts – rooms. With the return journey we come at daybreak past the third halt; then I can throw you off and at least you won't get there in the bloody dark. With all those weeds you'd never in a million years find that house in the dark!"

But Delport preferred to disembark. He was in a hurry for Ann to be able to rest.

"For all that you know, the house isn't even standing any more," the captain said with a wide grin and cradled his brandy. "You don't know this bloody world. It's darkest Africa."

Delport just let him talk.

It was already dark when they got off at the third stop – Delport with the two suitcases, Ann with a few loose items. She had had that sickly green dress on that the crippled hotelier had given her that night in Catuane. The dead woman's dress.

The official in Beira had assured them that there would be a native at the stop waiting to help them and show them to the house. But there was no one.

Rodrigues hung over the railing of the boat and wanted to know over and over again if they would be all right by themselves, and

Delport assured him that everything was okay. And when Rodrigues was certain that everything was okay, he hung a little further over the railing and threw up into the reeds, blew his nose, waved and screamed at Pio that he could get going.

They were left alone in the dark and stood and watched how the Mahala's lanterns drifted over the dark water. Ann said they should go and find that house, she could not last much longer.

They climbed through the reeds, up the embankment, into an overgrown pathway and in front of them were mango trees and darkness. Delport walked in front and came to a stop at the place where the path forked. They searched for a light somewhere or a sign that would indicate in which direction the house lay. But there was nothing apart from the darkness and the silence, and in the silence a nightjar that called out now and again like a scared child, somewhat unsure, somewhat questioning.

He chose the right-hand path and behind him Ann said nothing, just followed as if she was sure he knew where he was going. The path swung back and forth between the trees and after a while it began to get wider and wider and then suddenly it was a yard – or rather, something that had once been a yard. No one had been living in the house for almost a year – the stinkweed and cosmos and grass grew in wild patches all over the yard. He came to a stop a short distance from the front door and put the suitcases down. Ann came to stand beside him and looked at the dark house and then at him. They said nothing and he looked for the key in his pocket and walked up to the house, went up the three steps to where the cricket became silent at his feet.

The screendoor was not locked, but when he went in, his face broke through cobwebs in the dark. He unlocked the sitting room door and when he pushed the door open he could smell the bat droppings and the mustiness of a confined place that had been shut for a long time.

They brought the suitcases up to the veranda and surveyed the rest of the house with a torch.

The previous owner – according to the official in Beira he was a bachelor – died of malaria during a holiday in Porto Amélia and they could not find anyone to take over his job. Everyone had misgivings about the isolation and they had to wait for someone like Delport, someone looking for isolation, someone who would be suitable for nothing other than the bush.

The official in Beira assured them that the house was still just as the previous employee had left it for his holiday: fully furnished.

There was furniture. But the back door had been broken down and some of the rooms were empty. Some of the remaining furniture was broken, and by then everything was under a thick layer of dust. The floors were black from bat droppings and there were wasps' nests against the walls.

They moved from room to room, following the searching spotlight of the torch which explored zealously at first, but gradually came to swing away shyly from the scurrying cockroaches and fleeing mice, a spotlight that became ever more unwilling to expose the desolation.

They went out on to the back veranda and Ann waited there; Delport had to walk alone across the overgrown courtyard to the outside kitchen. This door had also been broken down and he went in and was hit by the rancid smell. A mouse sat on the stove, trembling with fright, its white nose and little round eyes perfectly still in the light. And in the washing basin was the small skeleton of a lizard.

Perhaps, he thought, he should have listened to the drunk Rodrigues.

They did not sleep that night and at daybreak he stood in the yard and among the rusted fish tins and rubble he remembered another night, another daybreak.

The night in Ritter's bungalow when everything had begun.

Delport's life was made up of such nights. There was the night with Ann in Ritter's bungalow, and the night at Ballito on the beach when he had rolled the warm corpse over on the sand with Ritter standing nearby and watching in the darkness, and the night with the strange woman when Ann could not stop bleeding, and every night after that until their first night next to the river in the dilapidated house, and the night when he had moved into the back room, and every lonely night since then.

And there was the night after Gonçalo's death.

At first glance everything appeared the same. The brooding

darkness lay over the yard, over the sweet-smelling trees and the
storeroom and the house. And there were tom-toms somewhere,
and crickets; there were bugs against the gauze around the
veranda; and outside in the shadows, the child, like a blind
person, feelingly built his roads and talked to himself and
imaginary friends, imaginary enemies. He waged war against
wayward centipedes and unseen animals and wandered off and
among the banana trees whistled for the reed buck.

Ann slept under her mosquito net and spoke now and again.

The night's sounds were familiar, and its silences, and its
flavours. But behind all these things the mask hung silently,
unmoving like a dead face, and stared out with hollow eye sockets
at the water tank and the pawpaws and the storeroom's shut
door.

The rain that Delport had been expecting stayed away. He
waited for it like one waits for a person who never arrives, and
later he was not entirely sure what he had been waiting for.
Perhaps it had not been for the rain – for something else, more
unseen, more nameless than rain.

There was also no lightning. Umlenzengamunye was sleeping
or hiding away somewhere behind the mountains.

Delport lay on his bed in his room and knew two things: that
now he was scared of the mask that just the previous day he had
been willing to pay his last escudo for, and that he thought
differently of the girl than he wanted to – the darkness smelled
of her and he was with her in the back of the grey Chev and he
was scared of the dark.

Both of these thoughts were equally destructive, equally
disillusioning. Something told him he was losing his mind, he was
busy giving up. Perhaps nine years was too long.

He switched the radio on and the green pilot light was there
with music from Portugal. He let the light fade and grow over
other broadcasts, over monotonous Morse code, over faraway
voices from Brazzaville, Johannesburg, Lusaka, Dar es Salaam,
back to music from Portugal: a woman singing about love and the
sea.

He was standing in Tongaat on the bungalow's veranda. There
was music in the sitting room and Ritter was laughing raucously.

He was drunk. They could see, he and Ann, the six in the sitting room dancing – three vague, moving shadows behind the gap in the curtains. And the light fell through the gap: he could see Ann's eyes and he knew that it was time to leave. He and Ann said nothing, did nothing, just stood and looked at each other and he knew that it was time to move on. Ann obviously also thought the same. Ritter was nevertheless his best friend.

But just then Ritter had come out on to the veranda. He seldom drank, but that night he had gone completely overboard. He held on to the door and with his other hand on his hip stood and looked at them; his face was red and wet with sweat and he slowly swayed back and forth.

"What you doing?" he wanted to know.

Delport took his jacket off the back of a cane chair and put it on. "I'm tired," he said, "I'm going to sleep."

"Rubbish!" Ritter said. "We're driving to Ballito and you're coming with us. Come and have one last drink first."

All eight of them were in the same car and Ritter drove. It was four o'clock in the morning. It was not far to Ballito, but the drive was a nightmare of shrieking voices and tyres tested to the limit around every corner. They sat on each others' laps and everyone smelled of cane spirits; everyone was tired and a little drunk; not one of them really wanted to go to Ballito, but Ritter was the host and he had made the decision. He had had to threaten them violently to get into the car. He was upset about that and reproached them all for not enjoying his party, and he wanted to take revenge.

Delport sat in the back of the car and saw the telephone poles and stop signs shoot by the window. It was a dreary time of the night and he thought about Ann's mouth and cursed Ritter and thought: if you kill me in an accident tonight, I'll never forgive you. But all that thinking did not help at all; Ritter sang behind the steering wheel while the car swerved recklessly back and forth, chasing behind the yellow lightbeam of the headlights.

They raced through Ballito and swung off the road towards the beach, and the car spun around and around and came to rest at the foot of a dune.

Ritter went to swim, but the others did not feel like swimming;

they disappeared one by one into the darkness on their way back to town to go and find taxis. Only Ann remained sitting in the car.

Delport was afraid of staying with her and went to stand at the water's edge and watched Ritter splashing in the waves. His clothes were lying a little higher up the beach in a bundle on the sand.

Delport lay and listened to the song from Portugal, to the woman who sang about love and the sea and remembered Ann again like she was that night while he stood on the beach and watched Ritter playing in the waves, his big body a sea-lion in the dark water.

The radio played behind him. He went into the sitting room and still heard the music in the distance. He went to stand in front of the mask and could hear Rodrigues saying: The natives believe a man has three souls; one in the genitals, one in the heart and one in the head. The soul in the head is your guide, it leads you to the fattest bull – it leads you to everything you're searching for.

He stood and looked at the mask without seeing it; it was too dark. And he thought: that's what your problem is, Delport, you were mixed up with Rodrigues Pereira for too long. Ritter is not your greatest enemy; you carry your greatest enemy inside you: your second soul, because of the three he is the coward, the doubter. You are too much like Rodrigues, too little like João.

Even so – it was João who had wanted to warn him. It was João who had sown the doubts once again.

He put his hands out in front of him and in the dark felt around on the wall in search of the mask. His right hand touched the mbira's keys and released a thin note to reverberate through the room. He stood and listened to it, afraid that someone else would hear it, until the sound had completely died away. Then he took the mask down and pushed it deep under a cushion of the nearest armchair.

Outside there was already a movement in the air. It could not be felt, but the leaves on the trees rustled gently now and again. And the lightning did not sleep: beyond the edge of the earth it peered out once rapidly and then fell back again.

He did not see the child until he was right up next to him.

There was no moon and everything in the yard was degrees of darkness. The child lay in the shadow of the house, near the water tank. His game must have bored him because he had fallen asleep on the soft grass, on his stomach, the grader plank still in his hand, his arms underneath him, his head turned, his one leg slightly drawn up as if he had wanted to ward off something from his delicate body.

A while later he sat on his haunches next to the child and studied his sleeping face and wondered if it had been a long day for him. Then he picked him up gently to take him inside, but the child woke and did not want to be carried; he began struggling and Delport put him down placatingly and stood and watched how, half asleep, he ran a few steps away and, disoriented, came to a stop.

"Come," Delport said, "you must go to bed."

But the child just stood there, with his back to him, and did not answer.

"Listen here," Delport said and went closer, but the child ran away from him, further into the darkness. He was still not completely awake.

He followed in the child's direction and the child had gone even further into the darkness, ever further from the house, close to the river, his head big and unsure on that thin neck of his. Near the reeds he disappeared suddenly and Delport called out to him, looked for him, but there was no answer, there was no sign of him; he had gone.

Further along downstream there was something walking in the reeds, but it would not be him. Delport listened to its sound and decided it was a hippo.

If Ann had still been awake, he would have sent her to go and fetch the child. He always came when she called for him. She was the only person who existed for him, perhaps because he had never existed for her.

Delport followed the path back to the homestead. And behind him, without him really noticing it, a long way behind him, behind a horizon that was only visible for that brief moment, the lightning peered out and disappeared. The lightning was cautious that night, it stayed far away, it hid away, it lay like an adder around the world, tail in its mouth, at peace and omniscient.

And nearby the homestead the reedbuck whistled sometimes.

He did not want to go in again through the veranda door. The hinges were dry and he was scared that he might wake Ann up. She often struggled to get to sleep and it was just possible that she was already asleep; he did not want to disturb her. He headed for the back veranda, because the back door was quieter.

The radio was still busy making noises, interference and voices and smatterings of music pulled out of the atmosphere into the small ineffectual speaker.

He was on his way past the sitting room window when he saw the light inside. It was a pale patch against the wall, an oval patch of light falling diagonally on to the wall, on the place where the mask no longer hung. He came to a stop, saw how the patch moved slightly against the wall, as if searching for something – then he followed the beam of light to the lens of a torch, and behind the shining light it was dark; he could not see who was holding the light.

He stood and waited, saw how the patch of light searched against the wall, up as far as the buffalo head, and back, over the mbira, further away, back again. Then the light jumped to the side wall, looked among the other masks; and under the searching light he recognised each one: the Bajaka mask from Kinshasa, the helmet mask from Bobo Djulasso, the water spirit from Nigeria, the Baule queen, the death mask from Dahomey, the Makonde figurine on the table, stumbling under its heavy load.

The light swung back suddenly to the inside wall, to the mbira, where the new mask had hung earlier. The light stayed there, shaking slightly, as the hand holding the torch was beginning to waver, beginning to get tired.

Then it was dark.

Delport crouched down against the wall, and stayed there, crouching, and listened. He could not hear anything. It was a lonely moment when he turned round and went to stand at the water tank. He waited for the front door to open – he would hear the hinges. He stood and waited for it and he was no longer afraid.

He only felt slightly alone and remembered the night by the sea when Ritter had come out of the water. He was alone, because Ann had gone to sleep again and the child was somewhere down by the river among the reeds.

But no one opened the veranda door. It was dead quiet and everything was abandoned and it felt to him as if he was the only living thing in that forgotten night.

Was there someone behind that light? he wondered. Is there someone on the veranda? And if there is someone, what are they doing? Is he standing and listening; standing and waiting?

Delport looked towards the river, afraid that he would see the child approaching. But he could not see anything.

Then he walked round to the back door, quietly, and stood still under the pawpaw trees next to the kitchen, and listened again. He went inside through the back veranda and walked through the sitting room door. The room was dark and very quiet and musty, and in his imagination he heard the mbira's string twanging again.

He walked through the room, quietly, to the door that opened on to the veranda. Something was burning above his right eye, a little pain, like when you prick your skin with a needle. The pain became a warm patch, just above the eye, in the place where the hole in Gonçalo's head was.

He expected he would see someone moving in the dark, a long shadow. The shadow would swing upright and he would see a blue flame like lightning leaping out of the darkness at his head.

But nothing happened. No one was there. There was no movement. No sound. No light. He could only hear his own breathing in the darkness.

He waited.

Opposite him on the shelf against the wall were the three succulents in their pots, small and cramped in the darkness.

His legs were a little lame and he smiled without knowing why. He smiled and it made him feel better. It allowed him to carry on, quietly, as far as Ann's door. He could hear her sigh in the darkness. He opened her door, very quietly, and went in and he was suddenly glad that he was near her. He could hear her breathing and she moaned and the sound was comforting. He immediately knew that everything was good again, because she was near him and sooner or later everything would once again be as it was in the beginning; she would come to him one night and he would hold her against him and talk to her and perhaps she would cry or laugh or perhaps do nothing and search for him between the sheets, and he would sail into the forlorn country of her body like a bushfire and leave her ablaze, and both of them would not rest until all the insecurities and longings had been left behind, spent and unrecognisable.

He heard her groan and went closer, up to her bed, and saw her bent hip in the darkness under the net, and her white back. He stood and looked at her through the black circle where the net had been burnt and saw her squirming between the pillows, a body that had wrestled with an imaginary body, sighing and abandoned , shuddering and lonely, her hands hidden between her thighs.

"Ann," he said and pulled the net away from her.

She stretched and remained lying perfectly still.

"Ann." His voice was almost apologetic.

She did not answer.

He looked at the table alongside her bed and saw the torch.

"What do you want?" she asked.

"Why aren't you sleeping?"

"Leave me alone," she said.

"What are you doing, Ann?"

Her voice was hoarse. "I don't bother you when you're trying to sleep."

Mice were running over the roof, stopped, and ran again. He could hear one squeaking near his head.

"I couldn't sleep either."

"That's not my fault," she said.

He went to sit on the bed, pulled the mosquito net away and let his hand rest on her warm hip. When she did not stop him, he lay down next to her and felt her back was wet with sweat, like his face. The mice were running round again somewhere.

"Can I stay here?" he asked and smelled the musty air.

In his room the radio crackled monotonously between lifeless transmitters.

"Just go," she said.

"No…" He did not want to accept it. He wanted to explain. "Ann."

"Go!" she said again. And a third time, more quietly: "Go!" with a voice that suddenly cracked. Then he could feel from her back that she was crying.

He lay like that for a moment, her body near his and naked, and felt the bed sobbing with her – and stood up and went out on to the veranda.

Where the lightning, for a moment, was caught unaware.

Day was near, but still could not be seen. He could vaguely see the path and in the trees were large grey birds bent over sleeping under a grey sky. The creek was to his right and inaudible, but now and again he could see pools of water through the reeds and trees like a mirror in the darkness, reflecting hidden light. There were crickets alongside the path that became quiet as he neared and began their hesitant screeching as he was just past them.

He was alone in the drowsy pre-dawn, but he walked as time had taught him to walk: like someone who clearly did not want to attract attention – supple and yet hesitant, shoulders hunched forward a little, eyes suspicious under the eyebrows, out in search of something ahead on the path, head sometimes carefully turned for a moment to the left, sometimes to the right, arms almost motionless against the sides. That is why the blacks called him Inkunzinyati*.

He had crossed the creek before the sun came up, and when the first rays of light broke through the trees, he was above Mália Domingo's camp. He sat on an abandoned anthill under a copse of trees and kept watch on the path and the creek and the grey Chev, and then walked a little further through the acacia trees, around the camp, so that he could look in under the canvas awning. There was no sign of anyone inside.

He waited and watched the sun come up.

The night was over and together with it all the strange things he had been brooding over. The morning was bright and he saw

* Buffalo bull

birds flying past, shining wings in the early sun, and somewhere heard a partridge chatter in the dew-laden grass on the other side of the creek.

He must have been lost in thought for a while. Or thoughtlessness. But his attention was not on the truck. He realised that when he noticed that the back flap of the tent was untied; the cord was loose and the flap was open slightly. But no one was in sight. He waited a while and then saw the smoke – it curled thinly from the other side of the truck into the air, so thin that at first he thought it was his imagination. But a little later he was certain.

He stood up, went in among the trees and turned to the right, then walked closer to the creek in a wide arc, then approached the smoke directly until he could see the camp again.

She was standing alongside the fire. She was wearing a nightie and was barefoot. There was a kettle on the fire and she held a wash basin in her one hand. She was not aware of anything besides the kettle; she stood looking at it with her hair awry, probably for five minutes, and then suddenly, without first making sure that the water was hot enough, picked up the kettle and carried it under the lean-to.

He could still see her. She poured the water into the basin and washed her face, dried it off, washed her arms and dried them, then pushed the nightie off her shoulders so that it slid down over her hips and fell to the ground around her feet. She picked up the garment with her foot and threw it on the canvas chair behind her and with slow, indulgent movements washed the rest of her body.

Delport watched.

She was skinny and swarthy and small. Her hair was so short that one could easily take her for a boy. Only her hips betrayed her femininity and the small sculpted breasts that he glimpsed now and again. She was completely at ease and once he thought he heard her humming.

He remembered her as she was when he met her for the first time two days ago: tired and sweaty in her red dress; how she came towards him, out of the corner of his eye, her eyes hesitatingly fixed on him as if she was not sure she was doing the right thing – almost afraid, like someone used to being chased away. She was like a child, at that moment. He could see the child in her eyes and cautious shoulders. Even so, he was scared of her.

He remembered her as she was on the boat, later – how she, still self-conscious, still unsure in the face of his morbid indifference, tried to smile, unperturbed and tried innocently talking to coax him and to tease a spontaneous gesture or word out of him and so set her mind at rest.

He remembered her like she was the following day, in the camp, half asleep and unprepared, having paid her debt with the mask she had given him and therefore justified, in turn, to show her mistrust.

He stood and watched how she dried herself off while humming, at peace with the day and not in a hurry. Her complete lack of suspicion made him smile and made him feel guilty. But he kept on watching. Only when she tied the towel around her brown hips and disappeared behind the truck, did he turn around and head off between the thorn trees.

He thought about Ann, and her white hip pushed aside the chatter of the birds. "Go!" she said. "Go!" And her voice was bitter with humiliation and disgust and the bed trembled under them while she sobbed. Once again he saw the circle of light against the wall searching for the mask with the familiar face.

She had bought it from an Indian in Caipemba, she had said. And he knew which Indian. There was only one in Caipemba that sold wood carvings – a thin, dark man with brooding, blind eyes who had laid out his wares under a reed lean-to. The blacks were scared of him because they believed he was a witchdoctor. He often stood alone and talked to himself and there was always an incense stick burning on his table. It was Rajput who had carved the chess set.

Delport walked a short distance up the creek, along the pathway of flattened grass which the truck had created. The grass was already old and brittle and where it had snapped under the truck tyres, it would not be springing up again. Somewhere, he knew, the track would swing to the right over the creek, because the nearest road was the one from Colonial Coffee Growers down to the railway station at Dembe.

He went past a good many places where the truck would easily have been able to get through; the creek was not sandy and the banks were almost level with the riverbed. After half an hour, he turned back and walked back in his own track until about five hundred paces from the camp, then swung right and walked around the camp back to the path along which he had come in the morning. The sun was now high and it was hot and there were already clouds in the south above the mountains. He could see the heat dancing over the trees and somewhere where he could not look, the sun hung like a huge wheel in the sky.

Just in front of him was the place where Gonçalo's body had lain. He could see the patch of burnt, blackened grass. A hammerhead flew up from that place and, cawing, disappeared over the camel thorn trees.

Delport stood still on the path, then took his revolver out and fired a shot into the sky. Its sound dissipated into the plains and it was dead quiet for a while. The cicadas were no longer screeching and neither were the birds. Then he continued walking to the camp.

He had not yet emerged from the trees when he heard the truck's horn – twice, three times. He stood still. Waited. But it was quiet, and after a while the cicadas began their screech again hesitatingly.

When he emerged from between the trees into the open veld above the camp, he could see her standing near the truck. She was looking into the trees, then took a few steps forward and suddenly saw him and stopped.

"*Bom dia,*" she said as he approached her. "*Está bom?*"

He nodded.

And he could see it immediately: she was disappointed; she was expecting someone else.

"Why were you on the horn?" he asked.

"I thought it was my dad and the others. You were shooting."

"I'm sorry," he said. "I just wanted to alert you."

She was again wearing the khaki blouse and skirt, but she was still barefoot and her hair had not yet been combed.

"Just got up?" he asked.

"Just now."

It did not seem as if she intended inviting him to stay – even as he wanted to take a step closer, she remained standing and kept a watch on the path along which he had just come.

"They're not coming," she said.

"They'll come."

She looked at him and there was a strange furrow of concern between her eyes which he had not seen previously. "I don't know any more," she said without emotion.

"They will come," he said again, hopeless and not expecting her sudden abandonment of hope. A moment earlier she had been detached from him and inaccessible, and now it was different – completely. He suspected that she was sorry about that, sorry for the weak moment, but it was too late. They stood looking at each other in the shimmering light and Delport could feel the sweat creeping through his eyebrows and it was as if he heard her say again: "I don't know any more." But the furrow of concern between her eyes had disappeared and now she was aware of him.

I watched you. That is what he wanted to say. Perhaps they are not coming any more, but I did come and I saw how you washed yourself with the blue basin and I saw your browned body and last night you were in the wind around the house and I could smell your shoulders in the darkness. He wanted to say it, but could not, because he could not believe it himself. There was no reason for him to believe it. He had given everything in exchange for Ann, and even though Ann had not played along, that made no difference to things at all. A person can only give so much, then there is nothing left to give.

This woman had appeared here coincidentally; that is why he was just a coincidence to her. That is what they were to each other. That they were both waiting for someone who failed to turn up was equally coincidental and not important or lasting enough to mean anything. But he was not seeking anything lasting – that he also knew. He was not in search of anything of meaning. He just wanted to forget Ann's detachment. As it was, he had enough to have doubts about.

Under the lean-to his eyes searched for the basin. It was on the fold-up table. The nightie was no longer on the chair where she had thrown it. The washcloth was hanging on a nail against the truck's side and it was damp.

CHRIS BARNARD

She invited him to sit and then began to tidy up the table, but her attention was elsewhere. She picked a mug up and then put it down again; she took the washbasin and looked for a place to put it away and then put it down on the table again and she packed the paper bags with the sugar and tea and flour and salt, standing among the mugs and spoons and tin plates, neatly in a row on the back edge of the table. Then she picked up the basin again and put it on the truck's tailgate. He watched her while she did all of this and he could see she was working while her mind was elsewhere. She looked outside intermittently and a few times she remained standing like that for a long while. Her movements were sluggish and uncertain and she was once again barely aware of him.

"Have you had anything to eat, *senhor*?" she asked after a while.

He shook his head and then realised she was not looking at him and said: "No."

"Me neither." Then she went to sit down and looked away towards the creek and forgot about him.

"My name is Max," he said.

She nodded. "I know." But she did not look at him, just remained staring straight ahead, pensively.

"What do you do during the day to pass the time?" he asked a little later.

"Nothing," she said. "I wait."

"You must do something. Do you read?"

She shook her head, and then after a while, said: "I go walking. Sometimes." And then again: "There are lots of chameleons around the camp here; I play with them. But I can't find a lizard anywhere; I like lizards." She suddenly turned garrulous, but he could see it was just for the sake of something to say. "Yesterday, I found a hammerhead nest up there, in one of the acacias. It's amazing how strong they build those nests. It must be months of work."

"What else do you do?"

"I dance."

When he did not answer, she smiled and pointed out an upright wait-a-bit thorn bush near the creek. "See that bush? That's my clock. Its shadow tells me exactly what time it is. Sometimes, when I'm bored, I dance all around it. Round and round and round."

86

He did not react – just asked after a while: "Do you still have enough of everything? Have you got meat?"

"I've got enough for two weeks," she said. "And if it runs out I can go and get supplies in Caipemba again."

"But you don't have any more meat?"

She shook her head.

"I'll see if I can shoot something. There are lots of impala around here."

"It's not necessary," she said.

"I'll have a look."

"How can one find out if something has happened to them?" she asked and he immediately knew that was the question she had been sitting with for the entire time.

"Something won't happen to both of them at the same time. One will always be left to come and raise the alarm."

"It's the first time that they've been hunting here. Perhaps they're lost."

He thought about it: it was quite possible, and he said: "I don't think so."

"Do you think we could go and look for them?" And then, for the first time, she looked at him again.

"Where?" he asked. "The world is a big place."

"We can try."

"Let's wait a few more days," he said. "I'll tell my natives to keep an eye open. I have a whole lot of them going out on patrols."

"You're the game warden here?" she asked.

He nodded and then smiled and added: "Fire is actually my specialty. I make fire breaks. I fight fire. I watch for poachers. I do wildlife surveys. I do everything."

"It must be nice."

He nodded. "Sure."

"You're South African."

"Yes."

"How long have you been here?"

"Nine years. About."

"Does your wife like it here?"

He looked up at her and stared straight into her eyes. There was nothing. "No," he said and looked at the nails on one of his hands: five eyes looking back at him. "She hates it."

"Why do you stay then?"

"Because I like it." He looked at her until she turned her face away, and then asked: "Did you come via Dembe?"

"Yes."

"Where did you cross the river?"

She hesitated for a while and then shrugged her shoulders. "I don't know. Somewhere." She attempted to swat a fly on her knee. "I was too tired to remember."

"Did the people at CCG let you come through?"

"CCG?"

"The coffee farm. Usually they stop anyone who wants to drive through their land."

"No one stopped us," she said and stood up. "I'm going to make some coffee."

He helped her to get the fire going, fetched water from the river and put it on the fire. She washed two mugs and took out some biscuits. He remained at the fire until the kettle boiled and then took it to the tent.

Under the truck, against the back wheel, lay two blankets rolled-up. He could not remember that he had seen them there the day before. The short grass under the truck was pressed flat and he assumed the two men had slept there before heading off into the bush. One roll was a red and a brown blanket and the other a green and a blue.

Would they have taken other blankets with them? he wondered. Without looking at her, he asked: "The shot just now – did you hear it clearly?"

She looked enquiringly at him and then nodded.

The coffee was too hot and he put it on the ground in front of him. "I stood about thirty paces beyond the place where Gonçalo was shot."

"Why don't you go and report me to the police?" she asked after a while.

Delport smiled. "You didn't have any reason to shoot him," he said. "I don't suspect you." He picked up his coffee again. "It just seems strange to me that you didn't hear anything."

"It was raining."

With the rain on the tarpaulin, and the thunderstorm – perhaps she was right. She could have assumed it was the thunder. He was being honest when he said he did not suspect her – but somewhere inside him was a sliver of hope that she actually knew more than she would admit and that she was too scared to talk about it. But he did not know how to say that to her – he would have to explain why he thought she was too scared to talk, and he could not think of any reason that would not focus the suspicion on her father. If he had to say what he thought, he would have to imply that she wanted to protect her father.

She moved slightly and when he looked up, her eyes were fixed on him. "How does a person become like that?" she asked.

"Like what?"

"I knew it from the very first time I saw you. In Caipemba. And on the boat. And yesterday when you were here. And now, again. You suspect everyone you meet. You don't trust anybody."

"Do you think so?" he asked without taking his eyes from her.

"Sometimes I think you're scared. Even of me."

There was a fly at her face again, like on the first afternoon when he had seen her. The fly buzzed around her face and landed on her forehead and flew up and landed again. She did nothing to brush it off, and remained staring at Delport as if she wanted to force him to react. The fly walked across her temple, down her cheek and only when it was near her mouth did she raise her hand to chase it away.

"Is that why you stay here against your wife's wishes? Because you're scared of people?"

"Perhaps I am," he said. "Sometimes. But not of you."

"Are you sure?"

"I have no reason to be, do I?"

"Do you have any reason to be afraid of anyone else – to suspect other people?"

"People are deceitful," he said. "You should know that by now. Even your best friend can stab you in the back. Even your own child."

"Haven't you ever stabbed anyone in the back?"

"No," he said.

"Are you sure? Absolutely sure?"

He was still looking at her. He did not like the way in which she had asked the question and, in her face, he wanted to find a reason for the question. But he could not see anything.

"I can't remember," he said, and immediately felt unhappy about the lie.

"Why do you rule me out?" she asked. "If anyone can stab you in the back – even your own child – why not me?"

He did not answer her.

A starling landed on the Chev's bonnet and its purple body shone like metal in the sun. The bird jumped forwards, on to the truck's mudguard, and its feet slid on the smooth metal and made it fall off fluttering and fly away. Delport sat and looked at the faded mudguard, at his shadow next to him on the ground, and searched for a way to pick up the conversation again, with a different direction, away from himself. But he could not think of anything. How does a person become like that? she wanted to know. Haven't you ever stabbed somebody in the back? And: if anyone can stab you in the back – why do you rule me out?

The questions were well chosen. Almost too well. She asked them without conviction, almost with divided attention – but there was a link between the questions that assumed secret knowledge. Because all three of the questions had the same answer.

Was it perhaps just coincidence?

He looked at her again and discovered that she was watching him, and even when he noticed, she kept on watching.

It was she who spoke first. "I wish I knew what you were thinking," she said.

"I was thinking," he said, "I was thinking that I wished I knew what you were thinking. What you know. What you want to find out."

She smiled. "That's exactly what I wanted to know. What you know. What you want to find out."

"Then there is something that I can find out? Could discover?"

"Not about Gonçalo," she said.

"Something else then?"

She leaned back in her chair and closed her eyes. Her hand moved to her face – an uncertain gesture – and fell back to her lap and he realised suddenly she was trembling. Her hand had trembled, and her lips.

"Something the matter?" he asked a moment later, uncertain, because whatever it was that had upset her, it was something for which he could not have been to blame, but even so he felt guilty.

"You mustn't come here again," she said.

He sat for a long time and watched her, a little confused – then put his mug down and stood up and went to stand next to her. "Why not?" he asked. She opened her eyes and saw him standing next to her and closed her eyes again, shook her head. He sank to his knees and held her shoulders and gently shook her, because he was suddenly, inexplicably afraid. "Why not?" he asked. "Why not?"

She opened her eyes and looked at him. Her face was close to his and again he could smell the woman in her like he had smelled it in her handkerchief.

"I don't want any trouble," she said.

"What sort of trouble?"

He could see every detail of her face. It was as if he was looking through a telescope at something that he had always had to look at from afar, and he was amazed at every little detail. There were freckles under her eyes and brown spots in her black eyes and fine hairs under the red curve of her bottom lip.

"You must go," she said and the corners of her mouth curled like those of a child about to cry. But she was no child. She was a woman and the second one not to want him near her. But her eyes were different to Ann's – her eyes were those of a cornered animal. Her eyes were those of the zebra of the previous day, black and crazed with fear. And it was as if he suddenly woke up on his knees in front of her and for the first time knew without a doubt that she was more than the scent of a handkerchief, more than a cherished thought.

That afternoon, when he eventually found the impala and aimed his rifle at a fat female on the edge of the herd, he had still not grasped it. He wondered over the trembling rifle sights how one explained something like that. Something in him that morning had warned him that he was not right for her – and he was still not sure of the alternative. The feeling was always still there, after everything, that she looked down on him and was just using him. That final moment when he was on his knees and looking at her, he had suspected it, and yet he could not stop himself. She was afraid of him and he had not known that anyone could be afraid of him. And when he knew that, in spite of her aloofness he did the inevitable, last thing left for him to do. He pulled her down, chair and all, on to the ground and she fell on top of him, her face against his neck, together with her half filled mug of coffee. He waited for the moment when she would begin to resist, because he knew she would, and at the same time he also knew that if she did, it would be for appearances because she was just aloof and afraid of him because she was so young and perhaps had never kissed before. He waited for the moment when she would fight back. Her hair was in his face and his mouth searched for her face, and when he knew it was time for her to fight back, he felt the pain of her nails eagerly cutting into his back, and they rolled over into the flattened grass under the Chev.

5

There is a time in late summer when the veld looks new again. It is that time just before the summer starts turning to autumn. In each leaf, in each stalk of grass there is a hesitant colour which will later turn to yellow, but has not yet reached that stage; it is a ripe colour that wants to lead you down the garden path; it is a colour that wants to give the impression of fertility and growth where growth is no longer possible. There is something youthful and tempting in an overripe fruit – and in a woman just before she finally becomes old. That is what the veld is like just before autumn begins.

Delport noticed it again that afternoon when he walked back to the camp with the impala ewe over his shoulder. Blood was dripping from the buck's snout while he walked, and the drops fell on to his trousers and on to the grass. And the red marks against the grass led him to notice the colour of the grass.

It was the time of rains.

It was the same time of year that Ann had come to him. After the court case, he had avoided her because he was not sure how she would feel about how everything had played out. The three of them had been friends and although, as far as he was concerned, he had stuck to the truth, inside him there was still a gnawing concern that he had left someone in the lurch. Either Ritter or Ann or both of them. And nothing would reassure him that she was not walking round with the same concern.

That afternoon he sat in his bungalow and played patience with the rain tenacious and steaming against the windows and over the hills of sugarcane. It was Wednesday afternoon, his afternoon off, and they usually played tennis on Wednesday afternoons. It was not only the rain that made him stay in his bungalow on that afternoon. After everything that had happened, he was averse to people; he averted his eyes from other people – even his best friend's, because he could not help but see the questions in everyone's eyes. There was always that expression: where there's smoke... That is why the clubhouse at the sugar plantation and its tennis courts had become unpleasant for him.

Ann did not knock. Delport heard someone running outside and when he looked up at the door he saw her approaching through the gauze. She opened the door and only came to a stop, out of breath, in the doorway.

He hung her raincoat up behind the door and gave her his towel to dry off her head and then his comb so she could comb her hair. He gave her a stiff tot of brandy and they talked about the rain while she drank it.

Then she said: "Max, I need someone to help me."

"What with?" he asked.

And she said: "I'm not entirely sure. Everything is so upside down." She looked at him as if she wanted him to grasp something which she could not say. When she realised he would not grasp it, she stood up and went to stand by the window and he looked with her at how the rain hung grey and slanting and motionless over the sugar. "Ritter and I were to marry," she said after a while, and the rain was so loud that he had to prick up his ears so that he could hear what she said. Or perhaps it was just that she was speaking very softly. She turned round to him, with folded arms, her hair smooth on her head and still damp.

He looked down and picked up the cards, shuffled them in his hands and said: "I know. I'm sorry."

"That's not what I'm talking about," she said.

"I was hoping you would not turn your back on me as a result. It was either Ritter or me and I felt that..." Such words sounded hopeless.

"I'm not turning my back on you, Max," she said.

"You must say what you're thinking. That's your right. No matter what I was hoping for. Fact remains: you two were going to get married."

"It's just that I'm expecting his child," she said.

The rain sang in the gutters and there was a wind outside; it plucked at the screendoor and made the frangipanis scratch against the bungalow's outside wall. And then for the first time the reality of everything sunk in. Before that the night at Ballito and everything that happened subsequently was little more than a nightmare. The news of the child jolted him awake and made him realise and finally accept that it was no dream.

"Does he know?" he asked.

She nodded.

"It will make everything even more difficult for him," he said after a while.

She turned round again, looked out into the rain. "That's why we were going to marry," she said. "We had no choice."

He put the cards down. "Ritter wanted to get married," he remarked more to himself. "He would have wanted to, even if it had not happened."

"Yes, he did." She nodded. "And because he wanted to, probably would have – eventually. You know him."

"And you?"

"I don't know. Sometimes I wanted to. Sometimes I was scared. I never knew. But then this happened…"

He could not decide if by 'this' she meant her pregnancy or the night at Ballito. And he did not want to ask. Or perhaps it was just that he did not get a chance to ask. Because she suddenly said: "You must help me, Max!"

Everything began there. At that moment.

He often wondered after that what the first, the very first clue was to everything that was to follow. Sometimes he thought that it was the night at Ballito. But he could locate it even further back. There was the day when Ritter introduced Ann to him, because before the night at Ballito there was already a clue as to what would follow.

It could have begun on the day when he met Ritter. If he had never met him…

But he would never have met him if he had not gone looking for work in Tongaat. And even that had a starting point. If he had not been expelled from university, Tongaat would never have seen him.

One of Delport's earliest memories was that of a sunrise over a sugarcane plantation. He could not have been older than three. They were on holiday on a sugar plantation in Natal. They were visiting people whom his father had got to know years before at the deathbed of a mutual friend. The memory of that sunrise over the blue sugar plantations stayed with him right through his youth. He had romanticised that memory: for him it had become a synonym for a carefree and untarnished youth and freedom and he often promised himself that he would return to that place.

The afternoon when he had to go and bid farewell to his hostel companions, suitcase in hand, there was a pamphlet lying in one of their rooms on farming in Natal. On the cover was a colour photo of the sun setting over the sugar fields of Tongaat. And when someone in the room asked what his plans were, he picked up the pamphlet and asked if he could keep it. That evening he had bought a train ticket to Natal and, two days later, he arrived in Tongaat.

Often, when he wanted to decide where everything had begun, he thought: on a day before he was born when someone he had never known was preparing to die. But even that distant beginning was also not without its origins. He never wanted to think about it in that way, but somewhere inside him he knew: there was no beginning, there were just consequences. There was never a choice, there were only consequences. He was never the cause, he was merely the consequence of every action. And it was a somewhat comforting thought because it relieved him of all blame. But it was also a hopeless thought, because it made a prisoner of him, which he did not want to be, the passive victim of powers that he had never known nor ever would.

He had wondered, that afternoon on the way back to the camp, whether everything that had happened could be determined beforehand. How does one sometimes know something beforehand, if it is not planned from the very start?

Perhaps Rodrigues would know something about that.

That final afternoon before they had departed on the riverboat from Beira – they had been like children that afternoon: he still remembered how they tried to catch a butterfly on the quay – that afternoon they had come across the red corrugated iron building behind the docks and a wizened old woman without teeth had invited them in, first in Portuguese and then in broken English. There was a small table and two chairs, and cardboard stars on the wall. She had taken Ann's hand, studied it for a long while and let it go without saying anything. She had taken Delport's hand, looked at it and eventually said: "You have strong hands, *senhor*. I like your hands. I like your fingers. Look at the nails. But your hands are strangers to each other. The sun runs through your right hand and the moon through your left hand. You must be careful. You must remember: these are hands of the same body."

He had asked: "Do you know beforehand what is going to happen to people? Is it written in their hands?"

And she had nodded.

"Are good or bad things going to happen to me?" he had asked in a moment of audaciousness.

And she had laughed and said: "What is good, *senhor*, and what is bad? It's the same thing."

Delport arrived at the camp at a quarter past three and Mália did not greet him. She also did not comment on the buck, but came to stand next to him in the cool of the mahogany where he was cutting up the buck. She watched how he cut open the skin from the chest and abdomen and peeled it off the ribs until the carcase was a bloody red thing with fine veins and membranes of fat. He worked without saying a word, cut open the abdomen and pulled out the warm intestines, and was constantly thinking of a few hours earlier behind the grey Chev with her body so complete and intact, the blood nearby and invisible and painlessly present under the soft skin. Mália shivered when he scraped out the warm organs with his hand so that it fell bloodily over his knee, and he saw her turn away and walk back to the shelter of the lean-to.

He cut the meat into pieces and salted it and packed it into the damp charcoal fridge built under the truck. Then, for the first time again after he had left her dozing in the darkness of the truck's canopy to go and hunt the buck, there was nothing more with which he could keep himself busy. She sat near him in the deckchair where everything had begun that morning and she looked at him like someone intently watching an ant crawling over their hand. Her hair was brushed and her face, for the first time that day, was made up. She had the same clothes on as in the morning. And she was a child again and innocent and detached, like that morning.

And that is how he remembered her on the way back under the low twilight, alone on the path, gun over the shoulder, on the way to the gulf and silence of his homestead. He remembered her eyes that barely knew him still, and her relief when he greeted her.

Something grew inside him as he got ever closer to the house. The joy of everything was past and with every step increasingly he doubted everything except that one thing growing in him. Uncertainty.

He knew where he would find her. Her bedroom door was open, but when he knocked there was no answer. With his hands cupped against his eyes he peered through the mould-green gauze and did not see her. The bed was there and the mosquito net like a tent over the crumpled blankets. But the tent was empty. The tent hung crookedly on the thin ceiling cord and watched Delport with its black eye.

He stood back a little and then again saw the small hole in the gauze that was torn towards the inside. The points of the wire gauze all along the edge of the hole were neatly bent to the inside. He took another step backwards and then another. He wanted to line up the small black hole in the net with the hole in the gauze. But the hole in the net was suddenly no longer there. Only at a certain time of day could one see both holes, for the rest of the day the light in the room fell in the wrong place and you had to put your face up against the gauze before you could see inside. The sun had to be lower than the edge of the roof, but still above the horizon: about five o'clock in the afternoon. If you then stood on the veranda, you could look through the hole in the gauze and see the hole in the mosquito net, and if the net was hanging just right you could see the headboard – or part of it.

It was still too early. It would only happen in half an hour. Five o'clock exactly. Then the sun would set and the twilight would fold in around the house and on the child outside in front of the storeroom's open door and over every tree and bush in the silent yard.

He heard her footsteps in the house and a moment later saw her standing in the sitting room doorway with a mug of water in her hand. She got a fright when she saw him and stood still. A wisp of loose hair hung over her face and she brushed it away and stood and looked at him, her face pale and still wrinkled from sleep – but again, already, the face of a martyr.

For him it was as if he was seeing her again for the first time in many years. He recognised her, yes. He recognised her as the Ann that he knew; the shape of her face was essentially still the same. But she was much older and looked taller, perhaps because she was so much thinner than before in Tongaat. She was again only wearing a slip and her two breasts scarcely made use of the space which the cut of the slip provided for them. He could no longer remember what they looked like, but he imagined that they were tired and sickly and dried out like the rest of her body.

That afternoon he said nothing about her state of undress, because he recalled the red berries of Mália's firm breasts and the mouth that repeatedly called his name into his mouth.

He could see Mália standing bent over the washbasin and Ann hesitated in the doorway. She stood and washed her light-brown body in the morning sun and the tassel of hair again fell over Ann's forehead. She sniffed softly and ecstatically in the stifling darkness and her face was wet and salty and her lips were everywhere where his lips kissed her body, and Ann brushed the wisp of hair from her face for a second time.

"Did you sleep?" he asked.

She nodded.

"In pain?"

"The heat," she said. "It makes it worse."

He moved closer to her. He wanted to go past her to his room. He no longer wanted to see her and the abhorrence in him was strange, because it was an abhorrence that was also of himself. He moved right up to her, but she did not move out of his way.

"I want to get past," he said.

She hesitated for a moment longer and then moved away from the door and let him go past. But she did not get as far as the three succulents that she was originally aiming for. She turned round to face him and he suddenly suspected that something was wrong. He stood still and said, without looking at her: "You must get away from here."

"Where to?"

"Just for a while."

"Where to?"

"Wherever you want."

"I don't want to go anywhere."

"And nor do you want to stay here."

She did not answer, just stood and looked at him, the mug of water still in her hands. He could not grasp it – there was no sign of her usual somnambulistic lack of interest; all her attention was focused on him; she was utterly aware of him.

He looked away from her, into the sitting room – and saw the mask lying on the floor, in front of the chair on which he had put it. And then he knew.

"Go and water your plants," he said a moment later. But she did not react. And when he looked at her he knew that he had not misjudged the mask that first day on the boat. She had also recognised him.

He recalled the green stain on the windowpane and tried to convince himself for a second that it was not there but, when he looked, he saw the water tank's ribs undulating behind the stain.

"What's it doing there?" he asked.

"What?"

"The mask."

"I was looking at it."

"Why?" he asked. "You never look at the others."

"Where did you get it?"

"Bought it." He looked at her. "I bought it."

Then, with the subsequent silence just long enough, she asked: "Why?" And with that she finally betrayed herself. If there had not been someone like Ritter, it would have been an idiotic question to ask. He came home with new masks quite frequently. That she had found it necessary to ask him about this mask pushed aside any remaining doubts. But it was just that which forced him to pretend the exact opposite.

"I took a liking to it," he said.

"Then why did you take it down again?"

"I wanted to look at it."

"You hid it away."

He knew: they are hiding away from each other, each of them talking from behind their own mask of innocence. But they speak of the same anxiety, the same threat.

"I put it away," he said. "And you looked for it. Until you found it." She looked at him, without answering. And he could see how the membrane drew over her eyes again, how she turned around and began watering the three flowerpots. He wanted to say: I saw how you were looking with the torch last night. And I heard, just now, how you dropped the mask when you heard me come in. But he was scared of saying it. He preferred to remain silent and hide away behind his silence and spy on her from there while she continued what she was doing, unaware of anything else.

But she said, suddenly, while he was watching her: "You didn't buy it – someone made it for you."

He did not grasp what she was saying.

"Don't deny it," she said. "You had it made"

"Why do you say that?"

Her back was still turned to him when she said: "It's your face."

"My face?"

He looked down at the mask, then at her back, at the mask again.

"Did you think I wouldn't notice it?"

"It's not my face," he said.

"It's your mouth. Your eye sockets. Your forehead. Everything."

That is weird, he thought. She was taking the mickey out of him, or testing him, because the mask was an exact replica of Ritter's face – and especially the mouth, especially the eye sockets, the high forehead.

He wanted to pick the mask up and hang it on the wall where it had been earlier and go to his room, but she unexpectedly spoke again. "Would you like me to leave?" she asked.

He stood and stared at her back, weighed up the question, and, almost relieved, wondered: is it still the victory it would have been yesterday? She apparently did not intend it as a victory; perhaps she did not even see it as victory – after all, he did suggest that she leave, albeit only temporarily. Previously, when they could still talk now and again, they often lay at night and considered the possibility that she go away for a while, for her health, for all sorts of valid reasons. But then there were excuses, an endless string of them. Excuses that both of them embellished together. Some were valid, but as if the valid ones were not enough, they also made up others. The actual reason – Ritter – was not mentioned by either of them.

But when the bats began returning, and the brooding mould, and the silence, then the nightly conversations became scarcer, and more matter-of-fact. Until eventually there were no conversations any longer. She would stay, to emphasise her absence.

"I don't know anyone there any more," she said.

Is there any place where she still knows someone? he wondered. Which 'there' did she have in mind? She referred to 'there' as if she had forgotten the names of all the other places except for that one nameless place where she was.

"You can go if you wish," he said.

He looked at the furniture in front of him, the two armchairs, the bench, the upright chair, the Makonde carving with the hump and the mbira, and wondered: why does she ask that – why does she talk now about it again, all of a sudden? Did something happen? Does she know something?

Had someone perhaps been here? Did someone perhaps yesterday, today, just now sit in one of those chairs and chat with her?

Then he picked the mask up and hung it on the wall where it had been, but without looking at the face. He opened a bottle of whisky and poured himself a tot, went out on to the back veranda towards his room, and saw a thousand things that had not been there before – the stinkweed against the outside wall, the broken panes in the kitchen window, the torn gauze on the veranda. In his room there was a familiar smell which he instinctively did not like. Was it bat droppings?

Delport went to lie on the bed and felt how the sweat ran down his face. He was shivering a little and he could feel the blood pulsating in his temples. He recalled the buck's warm intestines and Mália's body. Somewhere in his head he heard Ann say she was lonely. "Don't you realise it, Max?" she said. "Why don't you understand that?"

Ritter stood in the bungalow's doorway, his one hand in the pocket of his bush jacket, and said something.

He ran out into the rain with the sound of shattering glass in his ears and the rain lukewarm in his face and he could not decide where he was going. He kept on thinking: it is going to go on forever; this is just the beginning; it is going to go on and on and on until Ritter gets near enough to shoot. He knew Ritter; he knew him better than anyone else; better than Ann. He knew that Ritter would not give up.

Ritter hated easily. He liked hating. And everyone knew that and everyone was scared of him – even those who had no reason to be. He was always friendly. He was courteous. He did everything with a smile. He was always smiling. That night at Ballito as well. But everyone knew that behind that smile a fire was smouldering.

They had played darts in a club that night. Shanghai. He was the new kid then. It was the first time that he had been to the club. He was good at darts and he had proved it again that night. He beat everyone and they had said, never mind, our champion is not here tonight – wait until he gets here. He had arrived at ten o'clock and everyone had cavorted around him like puppies and licked him and wagged their tails and begged him to come and show the new kid how it was done. He was a lanky man, tall and thin, with a square face and heavy eye sockets; he paid no attention to anyone and drank his beer. Then, later, he stood up and came closer and they introduced him as Ritter.

"I hear you're good," the lanky man said and took the darts from Delport's hand and threw all three into the One and turned around and said: "Three-nil."

Everyone was quiet and came to stand behind them. Delport knew what was happening. He could see they all fawned on the lanky guy and something warned him that it would probably be best to have him as a friend. They cheered when Ritter had a good throw and were silent if Delport did the same.

But on the Five, Delport threw a Shanghai. He was one point ahead.

"Let's put a beer on the second round," Ritter said.

Delport nodded. "But we're only drinking when we've finished playing," he said. "I get light-headed quickly."

He won the second round as well.

"Two beers on the third round," Ritter said and took the darts and threw a single and two triples on the One. Ritter won the round.

After that they remained head to head, with Ritter just one point behind the whole time. Later there were eighteen beers on the game. Then, eventually, they were tied.

"Last round," Ritter said. "Forget the beers. Let's put fifty rand on it."

"I don't have fifty rand."

Everyone except Ritter laughed. "Chicken," Delport heard them saying here and there. "Big talker. Look who's getting cold feet."

"I'll put a hundred rand on," Ritter said and took the darts. "A hundred against your fifty."

Delport heard himself take a breath, it was so quiet. Everyone stood and watched him. Not Ritter. He was quite unperturbed. But Delport knew there was more than money on the table; he could see it in everyone's eyes, except Ritter's. After the first turn, Ritter was two points ahead. After the second, they were tied. After the third, Ritter was three behind. After the fourth, Ritter was seven behind. Delport could feel the eyes. But it did not bother him. After the fifth, he was twelve ahead. After the sixth, he led with eighteen points. Ritter's first two darts on the Seven were in the section, but the third was a triple; Ritter was suddenly seventeen points ahead. But Delport had still to take his last turn.

Then, for the first time, he saw Ritter's eyes. Ritter was smiling, but his eyes were emotionless. Delport's first dart was in the Nineteen. He looked at Ritter and Ritter was still standing quite still and watching him, still smiling, his eyes still emotionless. Delport's second was also in the Nineteen. He would have to throw a triple seven to win. He threw and the dart quivered to a stop on the border of the triple seven.

No one moved.

"Is it in, Delport?" asked Ritter.

"I don't know."

"Go and look."

He walked to the board and looked. It was a triple seven. The dart was a good millimetre or so inside the black block. He turned around and everyone's eyes were on him. Ritter's as well.

"Is it in?" Ritter asked. "Have you won?"

He did not have fifty rand to his name. He would have to borrow it. But the dart was in the triple. Ritter owed him a hundred rand.

"Is it in, Delport?" Ritter asked again. "Tell us."

"No," said Delport.

"You owe me fifty rand."

Ritter bought him three beers and they sat together and drank without saying much. After that they were friends. He gained respect for the lanky man with the square face and the slightly downturned mouth. He learned to like him. He learned to admire him. And for ten months, he paid him five rand a month.

He often remembered that night afterwards – and wondered: what made me say no when I knew the dart was in? Was it really cowardice? Was it really so simple? Because afterwards he had more than once seen how people braver than he had crumbled before the strange man's calm decisions.

And at the end of that year, when the sugar mills closed after the season, Ritter said one evening in the club: "Do you guys remember that first big Shanghai bet between me and Delport?" And everyone laughed and nodded. And he said: "He paid his fifty rand off. We're having a party at my place on Friday night. I reckoned it's all of our money – so I saved it up for a few drinks."

They were all at Ritter's party on the Friday night. And on the final drink of that night before they had driven to Ballito, they had drunk to him and Ritter drunkenly tried to sing 'For he's a jolly good fellow'.

Ritter had introduced Ann to him just after he had arrived in Tongaat; Ann was twenty-three years old and shy and sometimes a little absent-minded, but she could laugh as well and when she laughed, he knew that he liked her. Sometimes, when Ritter was burning the cane fields, they read together, because his bungalow was near the hostel. Ritter knew about it and did not mind. He was sure about Ann and there was talk now and again that they would marry.

Among the people of the sugar plantation, superficial abilities counted for a lot more than intrinsic things. Tennis counted, and how well you could dance, how many acres of sugar your team of workers could harvest in a week and how many pieces of women's lingerie you could collect in your bungalow. Integrity was not an issue; you had to be a hard boozer. A sense of justice was a sign of weakness. Ritter could drink and he was a brilliant tennis player, he was foreman because he knew how to push his people.

The girls thought he was wonderful. And with all of these things he showed common sense – if that is what it was; it could also have been instinct. He did not know who the president of America was or how to fill in an income tax form, but he knew how to use other people's knowledge. And he was a philosopher. He could talk about life and death in a way that made you think it kept him awake at night.

Delport considered himself intellectually superior to Ritter and so he sometimes also ventured to challenge Ritter in other fields, fields that had nothing to do with intellect. And because Delport dared to challenge him, he was the only man whom Ritter wanted as a friend. And because he was Ritter's only friend, he also commanded the respect of all the others – even though he could not drink, even though his tennis was poor, even though he seldom took girls out.

But even these very things made him acceptable to Ann, and because he was acceptable to Ann, and later even more than acceptable, she chose him as an ally that summer when Ritter was charged.

While it was raining outside that afternoon, while he sat and played patience, that Wednesday afternoon, she had come and poured everything out. Because the rain did not stop, she stayed until late. They talked and played bridge until it was too dark to see the cards. The dinner bell at the hostel rang later, but she made no sign of leaving, and he was glad without wanting to admit it. They sat in the dark opposite each other and he listened to the rain. She said nothing more, and when, later, he wanted to go and light a lamp, she asked that he not do it and he guessed as to why. She was crying and she did not want him to see it. He was also glad for that, because tears made him feel helpless, and like her tears, he could hide his embarrassment in the darkness.

They only spoke a good while later.

He got up from the bed and looked for his lamp in the dark, then for his matches. But before he could strike a match, he perceived Ann in the doorway.

It was she who said: "I want to try and forget him. Completely. I want to get married and try to forget that I ever knew him."

She was over her tears.

He put the matches back in his pocket. "How long have you been there?" he asked her. She had the dead woman's dress on and did not answer him.

"Did you ever love him?" he asked.

She shook her head.

"How long have you known it?" He went to sit on the bed. "How long?"

"A long time," she said. Her voice was tired and the words were barely audible. Somewhere between them was a mosquito's tiny whine. He listened to it, afraid that she would speak again. He was afraid she would say something that would make him doubtful again, something that would wake him up. He was tired and he wanted to sleep. For a while, just a short while, he wanted to forget about her.

He had said to her, that evening: "Why don't you go away with me, Ann? I've decided to leave this place."

Or didn't he say it? It was she who first spoke of leaving.

"Do you really want me to leave?" she asked, and it was that same voice again, the same weariness.

He just listened to the mosquito and tried to work out what she was talking about.

"There's already enough trouble," he said.

"How will it help to leave?"

"As long as we are here, we won't be able to forget about him."

"Wherever I go, I carry him with me. Something of him has remained with me."

"One can begin again somewhere."

"There's nowhere," she said "to go."

"The world's a big place."

She shook her head. "Very small," she said. "It's small. It's very small." It seemed as if she was going to cry again.

"We're young," he said.

"What am I going to do with the child when it comes?"

The child. Was there really a child? The mosquito whined around his head, circling his head, and he wondered about the child. What would they do with the child when it arrived?

"Max!" It was the first time in a long time that she called him by his name. "I'm talking to you."

He stood up and went to stand at the window, looked out. He wondered what would happen to the child and closed his eyes and looked at the darkness.

"I know," he said.

They stood five paces away from each other, he with his back to her. He felt how he was sweating, he could feel how it was bursting from his skin, and in the heat the mosquito whined.

"I'm talking and you're not listening."

"You're imagining that you're talking."

"That's not my fault."

The child crept past the window, bent over, whispering. He walked over to the candelabra tree and stood still, came upright, giggling suddenly.

"I don't want to leave," she said.

"You've already left."

"I'm alone here."

"Last night when I..." He did not want to talk about it.

"You waited too long."

He imagined that he smelled rain. But there was no lightning, no wind, just darkness and the child at the candelabra tree.

"I've been wanting to ask you..." she said.

"Did I wait?"

"I've already forgotten, actually."

He could hear the river more clearly than usual. The drums as well. Perhaps there was rain somewhere after all.

"I would have been able to forget," she said.

"You never forgot."

"I wanted to."

108

He wanted to believe that. But he was not sure if they were talking about the same thing. He only knew that she was talking to him again and that was almost enough to make him believe.

"I would have been able to," she said.

"You're talking."

"If we could leave together…"

"Where to?"

Very small, he heard her say. It's small. It's very small.

"Away."

"Away is a place."

Her words became increasingly unclear. Perhaps she was crying. He was glad. She said: "We can take him with us."

He nodded.

"Away."

There was a small skeleton in the basin.

"Where is he?"

"Somewhere nearby."

"I don't know if I'll be able to."

Mália Domingo was somewhere alone in the night. She was somewhere in the dark and damp night. Perhaps she was sleeping. Under the canopy on the grey Chev. Perhaps the smell of the rain was the smell of her body.

"I wanted to ask you why you brought me here," she said.

There were drops after all. He could hear them falling one by one outside.

"Have you forgotten?"

"Perhaps I remembered incorrectly." She cried.

When he looked around, she was no longer there.

The rain fell suddenly. There was no wind, no lightning, but the night was suddenly grey with rain, and droned with it. The rain wanted to fall all at once.

He saw the child standing under the candelabra tree, against the trunk. He was holding the trunk with one hand and looking in the direction of the storeroom.

Delport saw the grey Chev standing in the rain. She was small and naked in her sleep, her face near the open and dark armpit of her outstretched left arm. He went to sit on the bed and wondered if she had remembered to take the two rolled-up blankets out from under the truck. Then he leaned back, his head against the flaking whitewash of the wall. He could no longer hear the mosquito, and the screendoor closed quietly behind him.

6

It rained until just before daybreak. When it stopped, the water continued to run through the rusted gutters for a long while, dripped out of the trees on to the roof and from the edge of the roof into small puddles around the house. But when it stopped, the last hour of darkness was dead quiet.

Delport stood on the front veranda and looked through the screendoor at how the trees became detached in the darkness and floated in the gloomy haze filled with the chirping of crickets. Invisible birds called sadly in the wet silence and there was mist beyond the furthest mango trees where the river should be. The pawpaw tree's leaves were clean and almost transparent and there were large drops of light on the half-ripe fruit. The birds began to answer each other and a last bat fell squeaking out of the sky and disappeared under the eaves. Then the sun rose red and allowed a first cicada to discover the daylight.

Delport went out into the yard and found his bike against the kitchen wall. The saddle was wet and there were drops on the spokes and bell. He took the bike and pushed it past the house and as he passed saw Ann standing at her bedroom window. She was only in her slip and she turned away when she saw him. He pushed the wet bike towards the servant's quarters, but before he got to the banana trees, he came to a stop. Somewhere out of the river's mist he heard the hoarse whistle of the Mahala, and a second whistle, and a third. He looked down the path to where the first smoke oozed out of the damp quarters, but no one could be seen outside. Then he leaned his bike against the nearest tree trunk and headed to the river through the banana trees.

It could mean anything. It could mean there was news. It would not be post, because then Rodrigues would have let it be known on his journey upriver. The most likely would be that Rodrigues was bored and wanted to chat.

When he came among the reeds, he could already hear the thudding of the boat, somewhere in the grey bank above the water. But the mist was lifting and while he stood and waited, he could see the islands of reeds appearing one after the other. His eyes were waiting for the blunt bow, but he knew it would not come before the thudding stopped. There was a moment when he thought the boat was going past, because the sound was very close and still the diesel engine had not been switched off. But then he saw the boat looming out of the white vapour and it was still quite a distance away; it was the night's rain that allowed the sound to be carried so well.

When the thudding stopped, the sun suddenly broke through and drew pale stripes on the river and Delport astonishingly realised that he could see everything, that he was aware of every moment. He remembered the stinkweed against the kitchen wall and the broken panes, the morning's first birds, the bat, the sun rising red: something in him was different to before. But, immediately, he knew he was mistaken. He had also seen it before, but differently; before, only his eyes had seen it – now, his whole consciousness was aware of it.

He stood and watched how the boat drifted in to the pier over the idle water and later came to rest against the creaking bamboo railings. The six white painted letters near the bow drifted upside down in the water. What does it matter, he thought, to be able to see and to know, to be aware? To replace a windowpane and rake a yard – what does it matter in the greater scheme of things?

The reflected letters hung ruffled below the water and he heard Rodrigues say again: "It's an inexplicable word. It's like life. It's like the whole world. To want to reach the horizon – to want to flee the sun on foot – The good that I would, I do not: but the evil which I would not... It's something like that."

There were voices above him on the deck and a bustling, and he could hear Rodrigues giving an order between his teeth. Then the gangplank came down and the captain stood there, solid and calm against the morning light, the day's first hesitant sliver of sun on his threadbare uniform and his pale, proud, rank insignia. There was a three-day beard on his cheeks and a pipe in his mouth and a little blue smoke and a smile.

"You're early," Delport said and it was the first time since the previous night that he had heard his own voice.

"Had no need to stop," Rodrigues said, and his voice was also rough from sleep. "I'm empty." He always spoke of the boat as if it was himself, in the first person. And Delport understood it well, because nine years next to the river had taught him to associate Rodrigues and the boat with each other. Rodrigues's troubles were also the boat's; the boat's achievements were also Rodrigues's. Once, three years ago, when Rodrigues came down with malaria, Pio – when his captain could no longer continue – moored at the second stop and for six days the boat sat feverishly and sweltered in the forsaken river. Pio would easily have been able to step into his captain's shoes and take over, but for some reason or other this possibility was not ever once considered.

Delport went on to the gangplank and again sensed that fish smell and the flavour of Rodrigues's dry pipe tobacco. There were some passengers, a group of about six blacks sitting on rolled-up blankets and staring out over the railings into the hazy bank. But they were not enough to remind him of his duty.

"I came across a new move last night," he said. "Bloody simple, but no one will see it coming. Have you got time?"

"Do you want to show me?" Delport asked.

"I want to beat you with it," Rodrigues laughed and put his pipe in his pocket, and Delport stood for a moment and looked at how the smoke curled out of Rodrigues's pocket and blew away.

"Now?" Delport looked up and then at the six passengers.

"Pio has to transfer diesel anyway."

They went down to Rodrigues's cabin and the captain took the chess board out, began unpacking the pieces. The engine had already gone silent, but the boat swayed regularly to and fro in the river's stream and Delport could smell mouldy biscuits and Rodrigues's tobacco while he sat calmly and filled his pipe.

Delport was first to move.

Rodrigues watched him and, when he hesitated, asked: "How's it going with the girl?" There was a cloud of blue smoke around the captain's face.

Delport decided to create a space for his right-hand bishop. "I don't know," he said and moved, sat, and waited for the captain to take his turn. A beam of sunlight reflected, thin and shining like a new sword, through the small porthole and it touched haltingly, fleetingly on the sickle horns of the crowned bull. "Why do you ask?"

Then Rodrigues moved one of his front pawns out and said: "I met her people."

"Her people?" Delport did not look up.

"The two hunters. Last night at the hotel in Lotsumo. Two nice blokes." He snorted. "But, good god, what is she doing with them? She might as well have stayed with me."

Delport moved again – this time his open bishop. It was not exactly what he had wanted to do.

"What's wrong with them?" he asked.

"The one is her father or something like that. Looks just like a bloody butcher. And the other one has a peg leg. He says a buffalo caught up with him. Or a rhino, I don't know any more. How he can hunt like that..." Rodrigues pushed two fat fingers behind a pawn and moved it. "But he must be her lover or something, because when he got drunk, he told me how hot she was in bed." The captain sighed like someone who had let a golden opportunity slip through his fingers. "But I wonder – she didn't look much like that to me."

The sun reflected slightly on the ring on the captain's finger, on his shining medals and the threadbare patches on his uniform. They played in turn – Delport distant, the captain earnest, breathless, smiling.

"Are you sure it's the girl's people?"

The captain sniffed loudly and nodded. "Their camp is up there next to Dois creek."

Delport took his turn, completely uninterested, and Rodrigues laughed quietly and took his pipe out of his mouth and studiously put it down. "Mate," he said and placed his bishop in front of the bull.

He went into the house and everything was the same – so precisely the same that he did not actually notice anything. In the sitting room he stood still, wondering where he was going, and remembered that his wet bike was still standing at the banana trees where he had left it. Then he thought again about the green stain on the window pane and how he had seen the day's first light in the young pawpaw tree. And he tried to remember what he had been thinking of a moment before – it was an unsettling thought, because its aftermath was still with him. He looked away from the storeroom, into the room around him, and saw the mask hanging to his right. And the mask was crooked on its nail. Then he remembered: Mália's two friends in the hotel at Lotsumo.

Rodrigues's arse, he thought. That's a typical Rodrigues story: every woman that he knew or had ever heard of, was hot in bed. Ann as well, probably.

He straightened the mask and looked at it again, wondering how it had ended up so crooked. He remembered his bike again with the raindrops on the bell.

The next moment Fernando, was at the front door. They saw each other at the same time and both got a fright. Neither of them had been expecting the other. But Fernando was just startled for a second, before walking past Delport to the back of the house.

Something did not look right and Delport went to the front door and stood still. Ann was at her bedroom door, still in her slip, and when she saw him, she looked away.

It was just a flash in his mind: how long had he been in the sitting room, and where was Fernando, and where was Ann? And why were they so quiet? Why had neither of them said anything while he was in the sitting room?

He got that feeling again that had come back to him, in the sitting room, so sluggishly out of his memory. And he heard his voice ask from far away: "What were you two doing?"

Ann remained with her back to him.

"You're still not dressed," he said, and his voice was nearer this time. He took a step on to the veranda and saw Ann turn her face towards him. "What were you two doing?" he asked.

"You're sick."

From her mouth and eyes it looked as if she was screaming the words, but they were so soft that he could barely hear them.

And she said something else and this time he could not hear it at all.

The child rode past the veranda on Delport's bike, his brown knees churning, the bike leaning over so as to balance his twisted body as he pedalled at an awkward angle under the crossbar, raising dust.

"Why don't you get rid of him?" Ann said and it was as if her voice, something in her voice was teasing him, taunting him. "If you suspect him."

"That won't change anything," he said.

She looked away again. "I don't understand you any more," she said. "Nothing about you. I only know that you must be terribly sick. Terribly sick." She turned round and it looked as if she was falling away into her room, and from somewhere he heard her muffled voice say again: "Terribly sick."

Her room was untidy, the bed still unmade, the mosquito net thrown open around the top of the bed. She stood with her face against the wardrobe door, her lips flat against the wood, and he could see her whole body trembling. He stood in the doorway and wanted to say something, but there were footsteps somewhere and when he turned round, Fernando fell to his knees behind him, a step away from him, with a rag in one hand and the other hand began moving over the floor and there was a brush under his black fingers. And Delport kicked at the brush and got Fernando on the wrist.

Delport's pith helmet was in his hand; he saw how the black man on his knees swung away and came upright and stood frightened against the wire gauze and looked at him. He flung the pith helmet at the black man and the pith helmet hit the gauze and fell to the floor and hobbled on its edge across the pock-marked cement and came to a stop.

"What is it, *amo*?" the servant asked.

Delport wanted to be cross; he knew he had to be cross. But where the anger should have been, there was nothing. There was absolutely nothing. There was something like anger when he had kicked, when he had thrown the pith helmet, but it had suddenly disappeared and he stood and waited for it to return. He did not want to talk before it had returned. But there was nothing more.

It was quite quiet, all of a sudden. Very quiet.

And in the silence he said: "Get out, Fernando. Just fuck off!" He said it like someone who was cross. "And I don't want to see you here again. There's the door, there right next to you. Go on!" And he screamed in the hope that the anger would return.

The native looked at him a moment longer, then turned away, his black face greyish on the cheekbones, and walked out. The door banged shut behind him and Delport stood and waited for the bang to echo somewhere in the distance, somewhere in his head: everything was empty, suddenly – the yard and the trees, the veranda's gauze: everything was grey, like Fernando's cheeks, and hot and suddenly incredibly unimportant.

He turned around, just fleetingly, to Ann, and saw she was standing and looking at him, unmoving and dead and taut as a chair, and he walked up to his pith helmet and picked it up, kept on moving, past things, past doors that closed behind him, to his bike which was lying on the ground with its wheels slowly turning in circles and making the sun dance over the spokes.

He rode along the firebreak as far as the mahogany trees, west along the game path, carried his bike over the Dois creek and forgot to drink some water, went into the mopani brush along the hippo path, as far as the third firebreak, then followed it, further north, as far as the railway line, then rode east, along the railway line, examined the perimeter fence here and there, and stopped now and again to examine spoor, watch ants marching through the hot sun, and rode, past the bottom end of João Albasini's camp, watched some babblers, drank some of the night's rainwater in a shallow puddle on a flat rock, pushed his bike as far as João's twin-track road, and rode again, into the bush and through open patches of sun.

Near the hippo pool he came across a herd of buffalo. He stood for a long time and watched them – and they him. Each one was a horned shadow, under a heavy hump, a masticating thing staring blindly and not seeing, sensing danger and sniffing the air, fearful of moving first. They were a thousand eyes looking into the sun.

Only when he was past them and some distance away, did he hear them breaking through the thick bush along the creek.

There were images in his head, flashes of things, but nothing stayed. The morning was there and he knew about the morning, and of everything he was seeing, but everything that he observed fled from his mind the moment he left it behind. Ann was there, once or twice, and Rodrigues's bishop, and Mália standing in the sun and having a bath, and Fernando's "What is it, *amo*?", but a hornbill, a tussock, a few impala grazing, were each time more important than the remembered images.

Only when the heat became too much and he began pushing his bike tiredly did a complete thought come. It's not only the humiliation, he thought. There is something else as well. For a moment he wondered: what?

And somewhere, when he began riding again, he remembered: I could not get angry.

Then there was nothing again. Until he discovered that he was standing in the yard next to his bike, and he was looking at Ann's bedroom window.

Later he remembered how desolate the yard was. The kitchen was quiet and the curtains in her bedroom were closed. He did not see the child, but there was a new road between the frangipanis and the blue wind-up car lay without wheels in the sun. It was strange for him that he happened to notice that and remembered it. Because it was unimportant; it was an insignificant, small fact beside the hopeless realisation of that afternoon.

He stood in the yard, a few paces away from the back door, both of his hands on the bike's saddle, and tried to recall when the last time was that he did something of which he was absolutely convinced. When last did he really do something? When last did he do more than the usual routine things that a person does without thinking, without deciding, without having to choose? There was perhaps something now and again, yes, something that he still remembered two days later because it was unusual, but each time it was a deed of which the beginning, the cause, the initiative lay beyond him; each time it was something he had to carry out without any choice.

There were only two things – of all that he could remember, only two things that he could accept all responsibility for: the affair with Mália Domingo was one, and the second was the chasing away of Fernando. And of neither one of these two things was he convinced.

He had already begun to admit it: that he had become scared of doing the most minor thing, because every deed required a decision of him, and every decision made him responsible for something. And that is what he was scared of. And not just scared: it began to look pointless to him to decide on anything, to attempt to bend anything – even the most minor thing – to his will.

What does it help, he thought, for a glove to have a will of its own while the hand inside it makes and breaks a world?

Because Mália Domingo and Fernando – even these two: how much of what he considered as his share, was his share? Right or wrong. He had chased Fernando away because that was all that was left for him to do. Unless Fernando was innocent: only then would he be able to call the chasing away of the native his own deed, and his alone. And Mália Domingo – how much of what happened between them was because of his, and only his, endeavours.

There was the one big choice; the last one he could remember. In the small, hot courtroom with, now and again, the intoxicating sweetness of frangipani blossoms. Or was it even before that? When did he decide he was innocent? When the voice asked: did you see when it happened? he shook his head. And he looked up and saw Ritter's square face, and the face smiled, but the eyes were expressionless.

He could have said, yes, I was there. But that would also have been a lie. He shook his head and looked at Ritter's square face. And that was the last time that a decision was entirely his own. To take Ann to the Indian woman, that was not his decision. To run away, it was not he who had decided to run away. The morning when they read of Ritter's escape, it was Ann who said: "I'm not staying here, Max. I'm not staying here. Take me away." And he had said: "Where to? It won't actually help to run away." And she had said: "Take me away. God, please. Anywhere, it doesn't matter." They had packed two suitcases and it had begun raining outside. And then Ritter had stood at the screendoor with his hand in his bush jacket.

After that – what was left, after that?

Just finishing, the whole time; trying to finish, trying to deal with what had been started without his consent. Just running, without end, forever.

He shook his head and thought he was innocent, he was free.

Perhaps, he thought, perhaps that is what freedom ultimately means: to be a fugitive.

Then the decline was there. It was too slight to see with the eye, but he felt it on the bike – it went without him peddling. And he went past the patch of fire-blackened grass and felt he was going past himself. It was the clearest he had felt it up to that point; the previous times, it had almost been too vague to realise. This time it was too obvious to deny; he felt he was going past himself.

But later the grey Chev was in front of him in the sun and he rang the bell and, twenty paces from the truck, he swung his leg over the bike and rode the rest of the way standing on the left pedal. He leaned the bike against the bonnet and stood a moment and listened.

"*Quem?*" he heard her ask.

"It's me, Delport."

She did not answer again and he walked around the back of the truck, under the lean-to. And she was not there. There was a camp bed standing next to the table which he had not noticed before. Or had it always been there?

He could hear her in the back of the truck. He took his pith helmet off, sat down and asked: "You're not sleeping, are you?"

Again she did not answer, just kept on at what she was doing.

There was smoke where the fire had been made and he thought: she must have been up today already. He wanted to stand up to go and check how old the fire was, but then he heard her opening the flap and he sat and watched, under the back of the truck, as she climbed down the steps – first just one bare foot, then a second one, and then her knee and her khaki skirt. She came around the back of the truck and her face was red and sweaty, her hair awry. She was busy buttoning up her red blouse.

"Your people not back yet?"

She shook her head.

"Were you sleeping?"

"Trying to." She picked up a towel and wiped the sweat from her face, threw the towel on the camp bed and said: "This place! How do you manage to live here?"

She drank some water and gave some to him as well. The water was luke warm and somewhat bitter.

"Have you heard," he asked as he put the cup down, "of a place by the name of Lotsumo?"

"No," she said. "Where is it?"

"Upriver. About ten kilometres from here."

She picked up a tin plate and began using it as a fan to cool her face. "What about it?"

"Just wondered."

"But they told me that Caipemba was the nearest place."

"Who are they?"

"My dad and them."

"That's right. Lotsumo is not really a place. It's a – I think you could say it's a hotel."

She frowned.

"The boat goes there. There's a bunch of hunters there in the winter. In the summer there's almost no one. There was a trading store as well, but that closed down. I bet that the day Schwulst leaves, the hotel will close down too."

She put the plate down. "So what about this place?"

"I was just thinking that your dad and them ought to know about Lotsumo. They ought to know about Schwulst. Every hunter I've heard of knows him."

She shook her head. "I never listen when they're talking."

The middle button on her blouse was missing and there was a bend in the material and he could see she was not wearing anything underneath.

He looked away and asked: "The man with your father – is it a friend of his?"

"Enemies don't hunt together," she said and frowned again. It was an easy frown; her face followed; it appeared and disappeared like a sliding shadow.

"How long have they known each other?"

Mália looked away and smiled. "I'm in the dock again."

"I'm just asking."

"I got to know him first. He and Roberto only started hunting together later on. That was a long time ago."

"Years ago?"

"Yes, years."

"What's his name?"

"Bvekenya," she said, and then irritated: "Why are you questioning me?"

He smiled, embarrassed, put his pith helmet on his knee. "It's not really strange that I want to ask you about yourself and your companions. I'm interested."

"I don't want to think about them. Every time you come here, you talk about them. I want to forget about them. I want to..." She looked down, frowning again.

"That's unusual," he said. "You are here together, after all."

"Are we? Doesn't look like we are any more."

"You're angry because they're still gone. I can understand that."

"No, you can't. You don't understand anything. The one wants to be a bigger nuisance than the other and I hope they stay away." She stood up and began tidying up the table as if the matter had been dealt with.

"Roberto is your father after all."

"Step-father. Unfortunately. Or fortunately; I don't know."

"And Bvekenya?"

"What about Bvekenya? He's an animal. That's all."

"Is that what the name Bvekenya means?"

"You're a game warden and you've never heard of Bvekenya?"

"No."

She stopped tidying and looked at him. "He's the biggest hunter in Africa. The only problem is: he says it himself, too."

"That's a funny name. Is it his surname?" Delport asked.

"It's a nickname. It means 'the one who walks with a limp', although that's not what he says. He tells everyone it means 'god of the sun'. He thinks he's God himself and I hate him."

"Not really."

She remained silent.

"Bvekenya," he said and tried to think. "I have never heard of him before."

The girl smiled and looked away.

"What's his real name?"

"He has many names. Calvados. Jones. Witlinger. I think he's mad."

A grey lourie called from nearby and there was a slight shimmering of light on the horizon. And Mália Domingo stood near him and looked at him. Nothing else existed at that moment.

"What does this man look like?" Delport asked. "I've probably bumped into him. Is he small, big? Is he Portuguese?"

"I don't want to talk about him any more," she said. "He's Portuguese, yes. And if you've seen him once, you won't ever forget him."

"Why not?"

"He's a greedy pig and dominates everyone."

Delport stood up and went up to her. But she turned round, away from him. "Why do you stay then – if they're so... Why do you wait for them, then?"

"What should I do?"

"Why don't you leave?"

At first he thought she was not going to answer. Then, after a while, she just shook her head.

"Why not?" He stood right next to her.

"You wouldn't understand, Delport."

That was the first time she had called him that. And his own name was strange to him on her tongue.

"If someone hears you," he said, "they'll think I won't ever understand anything."

She laughed a little. "Perhaps you won't."

He pulled her to him, her back against his chest, and pressed his face into her short black hair. But she twisted herself loose from his arms and there was anger in her eyes when she said: "You mustn't do that!" He saw her eyes and her eyes were dark and moist and there was also anger in her voice.

He said: "Yesterday..." He dropped his arms and just looked at her.

"Yesterday was yesterday. I hate myself for yesterday."

"I'm sorry," he said.

"You mustn't come here again. God, Delport." She sighed and dropped her head. "Leave me alone and don't come here again."

The lourie was around again, further away than before. And the light was still dancing. He turned around, stood like that for a moment. And then saw the blankets. They were lying in a different place under the truck – closer to the front wheels. And they were rolled up differently. Previously the green and blue blankets had been together, and in the other roll the red and brown ones. The brown was now rolled up with the green one.

He walked to the back corner of the truck and stood again. There was a flat, round print on the ground in front of him, and further to the right another one. Then, when he looked more carefully, there was also a third and fourth print. It was like the footprint of a very thick walking stick. And the tracks were not older than an hour or so; all others had been washed away by the previous night's rain.

He did not turn round to her; he just said: "Bvekenya was here last night, you know?"

He could hear her turning round towards him.

"He and your stepfather were at Schwulst's hotel last night in Lotsumo. But they slept here last night."

When he looked round at her, her eyes were fixed on him. They stood and looked at each other like that for a long while, without saying anything.

The lourie was still calling somewhere. The light shimmered greyly behind her and over the trees. Now he could hear cicadas.

He walked over to his bicycle.

Climbed on.

Rode away.

At the place where Gonçalo had been shot, he wanted to stop, but something inside him made him keep on going.

It was late afternoon and the bicycle wheels' shadows were oval and fleeting over the grass to the right of the path. He kept on riding, even where it was stony and the path's turns were too sharp.

Delport kept on wondering: am I relieved, disappointed? Something in him was relieved that the thing with Mália Domingo had been dealt with. It was good, perhaps, in a way,

while it was still a vague possibility in the future; because then –
he still did not know why – it was reason for him to have hope.
But before hope had come, even before he could grasp why it
would bring hope, it was suddenly over and in the past. As with
all the other things before that could have given him hope.

He would have to work that out for himself: how one could be
relieved because you had lost someone who could have brought
you hope. But at Dois creek, while carrying his bike through the
water, it was suddenly clear: because you were already afraid of
hoping. Hope is good, until you learned it was self-deception ; and
he had had enough of that.

Disappointment; that as well. But was it for any reason other
than her young body? Perhaps so. Because when you think, you
hope no more, then the hope arises again; and hope the second
time round is more dangerous than the first – perhaps because it
is blinder.

And the night came in through the trees, very quietly, like a
great bird; initially only the trees betrayed it, the thicker bushes,
later the grass; and then even the path was barely visible. And
between the twilight and the dark was just a moment.

He rode fast, because he knew the path. He rode it faster than
usual.

Perhaps, he thought, she is lighting a lamp now. Or perhaps
she is sitting in the dark and waiting.

She had lied to him. That was the only certain thing. She
wanted to use him.

He rode fast on the dark path.

There was light in the kitchen. When he leaned his bike against
the wall, he saw Ann through the window, busy cutting bread.
She was wearing that sickly green dress. The one she got in
Catuana.

He went into the house and poured himself a glass of water,
washed his hands and face. In his room he lit a lantern and went
to the sitting room with it. He took a glass and went to fetch some
ice and poured himself a whisky, then went to sit in the chair
under the buffalo head.

There was something in the room that bothered him.

He sipped at his whisky and thought of Mália, but pushed thoughts of her away. But before he could, he heard her saying again: "You mustn't do that!"

The masks were in their places – the Baule queen, the death mask from Dahomey, the Bajaka, the water spirit, and also, when he looked over his shoulder, the one he had got from Mália.

"Yesterday was yesterday," she said.

How can you accept that willingly if everything you are has become past tense; if everything you do has already been dealt with; if even your future is so complete that sometimes just before you go to sleep you can lie and look back on it?

The chairs were all in their right place. The small table. The sideboard. The mbira was still there where he had hung it. There was nothing out of place anywhere.

He thought: you're getting old, you're getting too deep into yourself, you're beginning to see the inside as the outside. And then again: but there is not much left outside; what else is left?

The lantern's flame began to flicker a little, flared up again. He could see a cockroach climbing up the whisky bottle, very slowly, with feelers trembling in the murky light. The cockroach turned around and then fell and disappeared. But where it had been a moment before, Delport kept watching: it was right at the level of the whisky. He only realised it then – the bottle was almost empty, and it was a new bottle; he had only opened it the night before.

Then the lantern's flame turned blue and disappeared and it was dark. And in the dark he knew: someone had been drinking his whisky, and it was not Ann or Fernando, because neither of them drank it.

Somewhere outside, far away, a reedbuck whistled. Once. And again after a while.

There was someone in the yard. A noise. A movement. Then the wind sprung up and made the curtains pull on their rings.

He closed his eyes and smelled the rain. And heard it coming. Between the trees, in the churning wind, over the yard and the house. Until everything was enclosed in it. He stood up and went to close the window, stood in front of the pane and looked at how the drops broke, how each flash of silent lightning parted the darkness with a blueish tinge.

Delport forgot, for a moment, about the almost empty bottle: first there is hope and then a mistrust of hope; then existence without hope – and that is terrible: it is living without breathing. And finally hope arises again, like a second mistake: then you hope in spite of everything.

And that is even more terrible. God knows. That is the beginning of the end.

7

He saw her approaching from the outside kitchen through the rain, a lantern in her hand, going past behind the banana tree and in through the screendoor. He saw her put the lantern on the table in its own pale puddle of light. There was bread and butter, a jar of jam, a plate and a knife, a small pot.

When she saw him standing in the doorway, she said: "I made you some food."

He went to the table and sat down.

She and the child never ate together with him and there were times when he wondered if they ever ate. Dirty dishes on the table sometimes, when he came home in the afternoon, would set his mind at ease again.

He expected she would leave, but she stayed standing at the opposite corner of the table, watching him as he took the lid off the pot and dished up his food. There was neck stew and haricot beans.

She, he thought, had made it.

"Is the child in the house?" he asked and, when she did not answer, looked up at her, saw her nod. The lamp light caught only half her face and shone slightly in the three, four raindrops in her hair and on her eyebrows.

He got that feeling again: something is different. Was it Fernando's absence? Because he was aware of that all the time. He could feel Fernando was not in the house, not in the yard. There was no longer anyone creeping behind him and then suddenly next to him talking, no one that smelled like coconut and sweat and moved like a shadow and let the door bang.

But there was also something else, something more ephemeral than Fernando's absence. Ann had made the food and stood by while he ate it; that was something different. And there was the almost empty whisky bottle. But he looked past that for something else.

It was only a brief shower of rain – there was too much wind. Everywhere in the house – in the sitting room, in his room, on the veranda – he could hear the tapping of drops into the tins on the floor, and with the fall of every drop he could hear how full the tin was into which it fell.

Then Ann said: "You must get someone for the kitchen."

"I will," he said. "I'll send Kiya."

"Anybody."

He wondered where the child was, but did not ask again. The wind dragged at the trees, blowing a wave of dampness through the wire gauze every now and again. The lantern was smoking in the wind, and the blue lightning made the flame look insignificant.

"Why are you still wearing that dress?" he asked. "You do have other clothes."

"It's cool," she said.

He did not know why she remained standing at the table and he wished she would say something or go away. For him there was something wrong with the fact that he sat and ate the food that she had made, and he felt it made it so much worse if she stood and watched how he ate it. The fork reached his mouth with ever greater difficulty, became increasingly heavier, the food ever thicker in his mouth – until eventually, half finished, he suddenly put the fork down and pushed the plate away.

When he looked up at her, there was no reaction on her face, no sign that she had noticed that he was not eating any more.

And he could not do otherwise any longer. He spoke about it. He said: "What was going on between the two of you?"

The rain fell in sheets and he spoke loudly to make sure she heard him. He might even have spoken too loudly.

"Between me and who?" she asked.

"Lord, Ann." He searched for the words. "In Tongaat," he eventually said, "I would never have thought... If they had told me then that you would..." What he wanted to say, was hopeless. Talking itself was hopeless. It was so unacceptable to him that he was no longer certain that he believed it. When he spoke again, he did not take the rain into account – perhaps it was more for himself that he asked: "If you say that I am sick, what are you then?"

But she heard him. She said: "I'm bored, that's all. Is that a disease?"

"So bored?" he asked.

She said: "I'm lonely here."

The child appeared at the inside door and came to a sudden stop when he saw them. But his attention was immediately no longer with them; he turned his head a little to the side, as if he saw someone outside in the rain or was listening to something behind him in the dark.

"Only you?" he asked.

"What are we doing here then?"

He sat for a moment, then, almost unnoticeably, he shrugged his shoulders.

"He was in the house," she said.

"He was someone to talk to?"

"We talked sometimes."

"Did he understand you?"

"I don't know. He never answered."

There was a mosquito by her face. Her voice and the mosquito's were almost the same. The mosquito was near his ear; he could hear it humming over the rain.

"What happened then?" he asked, and looked towards the door – but the child had gone.

"He only ever kept on with his work. Swept. Polished floors. Made food."

"What did you say to him?" He looked away whenever he spoke – at an ant on the table, at a centipede against the wall trying to creep under a loose piece of plaster. He could not look at her.

"I don't know."

"And he listened."

"I think he did. I don't know if he understood."

"And then?"

"Then you chased him away."

It began getting cooler. The wind was suddenly gone and it

rained gently; he felt the air was cooler than his body running with sweat.

"Was there anything else?" he asked.

"What else," she asked, "could there be?"

"Something. Perhaps. How would I know?"

She looked at him, and he had the feeling, fleetingly, that she was looking at something she was seeing for the first time and that she did not know and that would make her shudder the next moment.

"I felt it," he said, as one defending himself. "His eyes. And you were always..."

It now rained very gently, fine and soft on the tin roof, with a murmuring somewhere in the gutters.

"There was something," he said.

He sat and looked at his plate, at the gravy between the bits of meat and bones that had turned cold under a dull brown skin. But from under his eyelids he could see her moving away from him, ever further away from the dull light around him.

"I knew you wouldn't be able to last." Her voice was distant. "I thought so."

The rain could barely be heard in the darkness, behind the gauze. It was no longer anything more than just another sound.

"What are you talking about?" he asked.

"He killed you because he stayed away."

"Who are you talking about?"

Her voice came from even further away in the darkness. "It would have been easier if we had not gone away."

And then he understood, he raised his head and looked for her in the darkness, because that was the first time in many years that she had spoken of Ritter.

But she had gone and the rain had gone and there was only the water running through the yard and in the gutters. The centipede had gone behind the flaking plaster and the mosquito had gone.

Delport stayed sitting in the dull light, stared at his plate of food, and listened to how the weather kept rolling over the distant plains.

Perhaps, if they had spoken about it right from the beginning, it would not have become so impossible in later years. But in the beginning it was something to forget about as quickly as possible. And because he could not forget and thought about it more and more as time went by, his willingness to talk about it diminished. And because she also kept quiet, he had left it at that. But that silence was the beginning of the mistrust – he only understood that much later on.

It was like a string of numbers that he wanted to remember, but was too afraid to write down. The more he repeated them in his head, the more he became unsure if he still had them right. He began to repeat them in a different order to see if they sounded more familiar in different combinations. And in the end, he no longer knew how they had been arranged originally.

There was the party at Ritter's bungalow. Then the hell-and-gone drive to Ballito. And Ritter went swimming. He stood and looked at how Ritter cavorted in the black waves and threw up small patches of phosphorescence out of the water. Later on he came to the car and no one was there any longer – only Ann was still there and she was lying on the back seat and sleeping. He began wandering around and looked for the others. He found one of them on the road and this one said the others had gone to town to go and look for taxis. And when he returned to the beach, Ritter was standing and arguing with someone. He tried to listen in, but he could not recognise the newcomer's voice.

The rest he recalled with increasing difficulty in later years.

Did the man try to hit Ritter? And when had Ann woken up – before it happened or afterwards? How much did she see for herself and for how much did she just have to accept his word? In court, she said she only woke up when they were on their way back to Tongaat. But Delport remembered it differently: somewhere in the confusion he recalled her whining voice continually asking what had happened. But Ritter confirmed her testimony.

She was still a child, then. She had understood even less than him. She was barely twenty. He would never forget that: her defenceless youthfulness of then. There were nights, even until the very end, when sometimes he felt that he just had to lift his hand and her incredible throat would tremble again ever so slightly under his fingertips like that first time he had kissed her.

Ann was a child when it had all taken place. She was not ready for something like that. Ritter was everyone's hero and hers too, and she thought that she loved him.

What was wrong with that?

Ritter was his hero too. They were the best of friends, he and Ritter. And there was nothing wrong with that either.

He liked Ann and sometimes he even desired her a little. And in such moments he was jealous of Ritter. Even that was no mortal sin.

But in the November of that strange year the sun had gone down over Tongaat's burning sugarcane one evening. No one had really noticed it. A couple of them had sat together drinking a beer in the hostel and then each had gone their separate way, to go and bathe, to dress. Ritter was one of the first to go, and at the door he had even stood still and said: "See you later at my place."

Delport walked to Ritter's bungalow at eight o'clock. The night smelled sweet and there was music behind the lighted curtains. He always remembered after that: when he opened the screendoor and went on to the veranda, he had seen Ritter's big head laughing, thrown back a little, and he held a glass of wine high in his hand, and Ann stood laughing in front of him, her one arm stretched out above her trying to reach the glass. But she was much too short and Ritter kept on laughing and ruffled her hair with his other hand.

When the sun came up, Ann was sitting in Ritter's car and crying – and he and Ritter were standing at a counter. Ritter was busy making a statement. Delport stood and, over his shoulder, looked outside, where the first light shone slightly on the blue roof of Ritter's car, and he could see Ann's bowed head. He could hear Ritter's calm voice next to him dictating, and he could hear a pen struggling over paper.

Perhaps neither of them, not even Ritter, had really understood what was happening, that sullen morning in Tongaat or at any time afterward.

How long after that was it – almost six months? – when he was almost startled out of the stupor that had begun in Ballito: the night in Catuane in the cold hotel when Ann became nauseous in the bathroom, her hands white on the bath's enamel edge while she stood bent and waited for the next contraction of her body, and the crippled owner with the sores on his hands and lips, who came in and, concerned, asked and kept on asking, later took them up to his room and looked for pills and in halting English told of the death of his wife the week before, and began unpacking dresses that had been bought in Lisbon, kissed them one by one and put them down next to Ann as consolation gifts because he could not find his pills anywhere. He let them stay in his room and when he went out later, Ann lay white and sleeping and cried in her sleep. Then Delport went out into the dark garden and with dogs barking in the distance and natives on the pavement under mottled streetlights sitting and chatting in the hot night, had vomited everything from himself, and kept on vomiting until he felt later that he was bringing his intestines up – his intestines and with them his entire being; he wanted to splatter himself and everything that he remembered into the dusty garden that night in Catuane.

By the dull light of his lantern, with the plate of venison and haricot beans in front of him and the rain monotonous outside, he recalled all that again – and again, like it was then, felt the sickness rising inside him. But he sat quietly, with eyes closed, and waited for the feeling to pass, then took the lantern and went to his bedroom, afraid of moving too fast, afraid that the feeling would come back.

He put the lantern down on the floor next to his bed and lay down: but, when he was lying, it was as if he was drifting on water; he knew it was the food that wanted to get out. He stood up and went out, into the rain, away from his body which smelled of sweat, and stood in the rain. He felt the rain sink through his clothes on to his skin. He stood patiently and waited and it felt to him as if he was swaying slightly on his feet; he closed his eyes and felt it raining and wondered if Mália Domingo was sleeping. He wondered what Albasini was doing, what Ann was doing, what the threadbare captain was doing. He wondered what had happened to Ritter.

Then his skin became hard and his stomach jolted and made everything burst through his nose and mouth. He stood with his legs splayed, hands on his knees, and no longer felt the rain, just kept on trying, kept on, until his mouth was bitter as gall, until he had to pant for breath. Then he came upright, tilted his head back, and let the rain wash his face.

In his room he undressed and sat naked on the bed, the lantern turned down even more, the radio switched on. There was nothing. Just a fire burning, deep in the hollow of the space. At first he was not aware of it, did not hear it, but later he began looking for a station, found a voice here and there talking distantly in Swahili, in French, then just the fire again – then, finally, something like music: a drum, strings being plucked, a voice in Zanzibar singing hoarse and high.

He sat and looked at his arms, his wiry legs. His skin was tough and brown and hairy in places, and he was thin. He had not realised before that he was so thin. Everything on his body seemed strange; everything was thin and hard like biltong. He could see his kneecaps through the skin, his shinbones, the thin bones in his hands. It was as if he was sitting and examining his own skeleton. And he thought: that's me.

It was quiet. The rain was over. He sat and listened to the silence and he could hear it settling. Through the silence, like through something tangible, now and again he heard a drop of water outside in the yard falling from a leaf to tap on to the ground, interwoven with an insignificant thread of the sound, his breathing, in and out, monotonous.

Later he got up, put on dry clothes, walked through the silence with the lantern to the child's room. The child was sleeping in a small bundle at the headboard, still in his clothes, with a piece of dirty string and the small plank he used to make roads, next to him on the bed.

Delport laid the child out straight, threw a thin blanket over him and stood and watched him without seeing him. He was not sure if the child was really there.

For how long had that been his and Ann's game – to have a child of their own! They had imagined him: gave him a room and a bed, covered him at night with their thoughts, took him for walks, taught him to talk, played with him. It was as if, with the imaginary child, they wanted to deny any other. But he never really became theirs.

Delport left the room and, for the first time in a very long time, again knew how empty the room was when he left it. He stood in front of Ann's door, just for a moment, and again saw the round hole in the gauze, and her room was just as empty as the child's: there was a shining thread of spider's web from the hole in the gauze diagonally up to the doorframe.

Then he pushed the outside veranda door on to its latch. At the backdoor, he hesitated for a moment – then also put this one on the latch. That was the first time in six, seven years that he had done so. He did not want to think why: something in him said it was not important, just because he could. But when he lay on his bed again, the lantern blown out on the floor next to him, he could still see his hand closing the latch. His body was tired and he felt a slight ringing in his head. Then he turned on to his side and closed his eyes. In his imagination he could hear the lone broadcaster's signature: four beats, three notes in each beat, except the last one.

Later, when he was almost asleep, he heard someone walking barefoot in the house. He recognised Ann's manner of movement. And now and again he was aware of the weather that rumbled in the distance. But eventually there was nothing – just a gentle scratching of mice in the ceiling and, far and near, bats squeaking outside in the wet trees.

First he dreamed he heard someone calling. Then he was awake and he heard the call again and thought it was Ann dreaming. But as he tried to fall asleep, the bicycle, leaning against the wall outside, fell over. He lay and listened and after a while there were footsteps, but it was so dark that he could not make anything out except the shape of the mango tree in a blacker than black outline against the sky.

Someone picked the bike up; he could hear the handlebars scraping against the wall. Delport lifted his feet off the bed and sat up, listened again, and stood up, went to the window. He began lifting the screen on the window slowly, very carefully – but before the frame could latch into the top notch, he stopped pulling on it. He could see the mango trees more distinctly now, and the frangipani. And between the mango tree and the frangipani, six paces from the window, someone was standing and watching him.

His face was against the gauze, and the top edge of the screen's frame was up against his face – so that he had to bring his head down a little to look under the edge. He remained standing dead still for a long while, his fingers still under the frame, and waited for the person outside to do something. But as nothing happened, he let the frame go and stood back a little. The person must have noticed, because he came closer – one, two, three steps, and stood still again.

It was a woman. Delport saw her legs and the line of her dress. He put out his hands and pushed the frame up.

"Ann," he said.

"Max..."

She suddenly came closer, up to the window.

"*Sou eu*," she said. "Mália"

His eyes were still not accustomed to the dark and he stood for a while and looked, then said: "What's wrong?"

"I'm sorry," she said. "You have to help me, please."

They were Ann's words.

"What is it?"

"Come with me," she said and came to lean against the windowsill. "You must hurry."

"Where to?" And again, when she did not answer immediately: "Where to?"

"I don't know," she said. "Are you dressed?"

He still had his clothes on, but he was barefoot. He looked for his shoes and put them on, then opened the gauze and climbed through the window and got down next to her, felt how her hand gripped his upper arm.

"What's wrong?" he asked again. "It's late."

"It's four o'clock. If we hurry, we can..." She kept whispering so softly that he had to pay careful attention to what she said. "Have you got a car?"

"What would I do with a car? Here?" Then he asked aloud, more urgently than before: "What's up, Mália?"

"We can't, here..." She looked over her shoulder, into the darkness, and let go of his arm and moved away from him, quickly. A moment later he could no longer see her, but he heard her somewhere saying: "Come!"

Near the pawpaw trees he caught up to her and heard her say: "I can't get the truck started. We must have the truck. I think the battery's flat."

"But what is the problem?"

"I have to get away!" She grabbed him by the shirt and pulled him closer to her. "They mustn't get the truck!"

It felt to him as if he were sleeping; he was not awake. And he wanted to wake up.

"Who are they?" he asked.

She moved around him, back in the direction of the house, and after a while reappeared out of the darkness with the bicycle.

"Bvekenya," she said. "Will both of us be able to go on the bike?"

She held on to the handlebars and lifted herself on to the crossbar and he put his arms around her, got hold of the handlebars and pushed the bike fast, for the first few paces, then threw his leg over the saddle and clumsily began pedalling, into the darkness, the bicycle suddenly heavy and wobbling.

Her back was warm against his chest and her head was in his way; he could feel her hair against his cheek. He got his balance and it was easier once the bike picked up speed.

"What the hell happened?" he asked again. He could not decide if he was angry.

"Roberto and them were there tonight," she said. "Can you see where you're going?"

"I know the path."

"Roberto and Bvekenya were there."

"They've been there every night," he said. "They slept there."

"They weren't," she said.

"You're lying to me."

She kept quiet.

"What happened tonight?"

"They're looking for you," she just said.

He felt there was sand under the wheels. His back was getting cold and he kept on pedalling and kept the front wheel in the dark gully between the tall grass where the path ought to have been. Because he knew every turn in the path, it was not too difficult staying on the track; he just had to get used to her weight. She was small and tucked up in front of him, but he was not used to riding with someone.

"Why?" he asked.

At first she did not answer, but he knew that she would, sooner or later.

"They know about us." she said eventually.

"They know what?"

"I don't know..."

They rode in silence for a while. The bicycle chain creaked each time he pedalled and he could hear the saddle's monotonous squeaking. In places, where the trees opened out, he could see the bush low and dark against the sky. There were heavy clouds on the horizon and not a star to be seen. But to the right of them, over the fever-tree plains, there was a dull glimmer. The sun was an hour away.

"They were there tonight and we had words," she said. "I told them you weren't coming back again."

He waited for her to continue.

"I never wanted to start the whole thing. I didn't want to come with them. But Bvekenya made me..."

"You're scared," Delport said after a while. "Of him."

"Yes." He could feel how she nodded her head. And then, later: "He was at your house today."

"Bvekenya?"

"Yes."

"Was he looking for me?"

"No," she said. "He knew you were out."

"What was he doing there then?"

"I don't know."

The grass was still wet and he could feel his trouser legs getting cold and heavy at the hems. And there were places where the water lay in puddles over the path; then the water splashed up, reaching over his hands.

"I think that's the second time he was there," she said.

"But he didn't want to see me?"

"He said he didn't want to see you."

"I have to sign your permits."

"I told him that."

"But now he's looking for me? About you?"

"No," she said. "It's about me saying I don't want to do his dirty work any more."

To the right of them a bird was startled and fluttered out from among the leaves. The bird swept by over their heads, so close that Delport could feel the wind from the bird's heavy wings.

"What dirty work?"

"I was only ever just a servant for them."

"Now they want my head for that?"

"Well, I..."

"You what?"

"I told them. With us – what happened."

"Why did you do that? You'd already said I mustn't come back." Because she said nothing in reply, he added: "The matter is over, surely?" She remained silent, and he heard himself asking: "Isn't it?"

"Probably."

"Then why did you tell them?"

"*Meu Deus*," she said, "don't you ever stop asking questions?"

Then they rode further in silence, and he kept on thinking: what is this the beginning of? He was still trying to grasp how he had managed to end up there at that moment. He tried to think about where he was heading, and why. But there was nothing to make of it – just one thing was certain: he was not looking forward to the rest of the path, that he really did not want to struggle to get that grey truck going, that Mália Domingo did not matter as much as he had initially liked to think. That hollow feeling in his mouth that he had the night before, the bitter taste that was on his tongue, came back again and he kept on pedalling in the dark path, kept on until his legs were hot and did not want to go any further.

At Dois creek he brought the bike to a stop and let Mália climb off. He stood for a while leaning against the bike, and looked at the water, at the gentle light on it. It was not so completely dark any longer. One could already distinguish the branches on the nearest trees, and the reeds in the water. The girl stood dead still next to him and he could hear his own breathing, the murmuring of the water, and a distant jackal behind them in the veld.

Then he said: "I know Bvekenya."

She turned round to him, but he could not make out her face. "You know him?"

"His real name is Ritter."

She stood close to him, and her face was turned up to his. He had the feeling she was waiting for him to say something more.

"He has a scar on his forehead," he said. "I once threw a glass in his face."

"Bvekenya?"

"Yes."

She shook her head. "He doesn't have a scar on his forehead."

"Then it's healed."

"What makes you think that?" she asked. "What makes you think you know him? Have you seen him?"

"No." He shook his head. "Not really."

"Then why do you say that?" She was visibly taken aback.

"Maybe I'm wrong."

Then he put the bike down next to him, sat down and took his shoes off. She followed his example and they went into the water and it was not as cold as he had expected. On the other side they put their shoes on again, he helped her on to the bicycle and they rode off again.

The day was breaking and he could see the path more clearly now. As they went past the place where Gonçalo had been shot, there was reddish light. But the sun still stayed away.

They only spoke again when they saw the camp.

Mália asked him to stop and she climbed off and stood for a long while looking at the camp. There was no sign of life. Everything was still.

Then she said: "Wait here – I want to go and look."

And he did not answer. But when she began walking, he pushed his bike behind her.

8

Everything happened of its own accord, after that. And, as before, everything began without him being able to understand where it began and where it was leading. He was at the centre of it all; everything turned around him, as around an axle, without him knowing where the wheels were taking him – without even the wheels knowing where they were headed. He was merely present, the pivot, and without him having asked to be involved.

This at least he knew ever more clearly, in the midst of all the nothingness, in the midst of the invariable coming and going of days: that he no longer really had the desire or inclination for anything, that the absence or presence of anything was no longer important enough to really matter to him. What he had done, from day to day, were things that half a lifetime's momentum kept him doing; they were reflexes. It was like ducking when someone hit you. He had done it without deciding if he wanted to or not. It was just done.

And there were moments, just moments, in the morning when he woke up, at night as he was dozing off, that he went as far as wondering: how did I become like this; when did it start?

But that was all. He wondered and left it at that. He saw no reason why things had to change yet again. It was, honestly enough, not important; certainly unusual, in relation to what had gone before, but not really important.

Just that: it was uncomfortable sometimes. Like that night, for example, when Mália came. He was tired and really wanted to sleep if he could. And when she arrived, he knew: in what was to follow, he actually had no interest, whatever it might be. But to withdraw from it would serve even less purpose; something in him wanted at least to try to hold on to things happening, something wanted to continue believing that even Málía was significant, in a way. That is why he went when she came to fetch him; against his will, against his better judgement, he had gone when Málía had come to fetch him.

Later on, close to first light, when he began to understand, began to suspect what it was all about, even in that one blinding moment when he remembered Ritter, he did not think of turning back. He kept on pedalling on the dark path, and did not know why, but pedalled, ever further away from the one thing he desired that night: a little sleep.

And as he pushed the bike towards the camp, following the girl, he knew for a moment again: he feared himself the most – not Bvekenya or the girl, not Fernando or Ann or Ritter. But himself.

Málía was five paces in front of him, but he caught up with her as she came to the truck. They came to a stop together, listened for a moment, looked at each other. Behind her he could see the sun's red mane stretching out over the horizon.

Then he pushed his bike further, around the bonnet of the Chev. There was no one under the lean-to.

"Come on," he said after a while and leaned his bike against the table. The blankets were no longer under the canopy. He came out from the lean-to and examined the ground – the only tracks made after the rain were his and the girl's.

"They haven't been here again," she said.

"What time did they leave here?"

"About nine o'clock."

"And you?"

"I only left after twelve. After the worst of the rain had passed."

The canvas flap at the back of the truck was down, but not tied up and Delport went closer and threw the flap open. It was gloomy inside, but he could see the two rolls of blankets lying on top of her bedding.

"Did you put the blankets here?" he asked.

"Yes." She nodded. "Before they had left. Before the rain."

"But then where did they sleep last night?"

She shrugged her shoulders. "Probably where they slept on all the previous occasions."

"Lotsumo is far." He looked in a wide arc at the veld around him. "Two hours' walk. Maybe more."

Some of her clothes were hanging under the lean-to and she began taking them down. "We must get the truck going," she said.

"And then?"

She came to a standstill and turned around to him. "We must get away from here."

"They won't do anything to you."

"Please!"

Her voice was deceptively calm, but her eyes betrayed a terror that he had not noticed before.

"Where do you want to go to?" he asked.

"I don't know."

"Can you drive?"

She stood for a while and looked at him. "Aren't you coming with me then?"

"How can I come with? I can't just pack up and leave."

The girl came closer to him, her eyes fixed continually on his, the clothes still in the crook of her left arm, and came to stand in front of him. He could see the bottom lid of one of her eyes twitching slightly. "They want you, Delport," she said softly. But this time her voice also betrayed anxiety.

"Why? I haven't done anything to them."

She swallowed and looked away. "I'll tell you." She swallowed again – he could see the small Adam's apple jumping in her soft throat. "Only once you get us away from here."

Delport stood for a moment longer and looked at her, then asked: "Have you got tools?"

"In the front," she said. "Under the seat."

The steering wheel was cracked and where the gauges should have been there was just a round hole in the dashboard. The key was not there, but she came and stood at the open door and took the key out of the front of her shirt. He turned the truck on and pressed the starter; it churned over lazily once or twice and then just made a clicking sound. The battery was already too weak to turn the starter motor.

"We'll have to push," he said and got out.

The sun was now half a meter above the plain, but the veld was unusually quiet; there were no birds and when he pushed the door closed, it was like a shot going into the plain.

He pulled the canopy of the lean-to away from the truck.

"There's more stuff that I want to take with," she said.

"Leave it. We must first see if we can get this thing going."

He did not have much hope. There was only a gentle incline to the creek – about twenty paces or so. If the thing did not catch in those twenty paces, they would be stuck. A second possibility was to swing the truck's nose to the right and to push it between the sweet-thorn trees to their right – from there they would have a good incline for about two hundred paces, all along the creek.

But how to get the truck to the sweet-thorns. The ground was level all the way there and the thing was heavy.

He weighed everything up for a while and then said: "We won't be able to get this thing moving. We'll have to go on the bike."

"We have to try," she said. "I'll push."

Delport wanted to smile.

"Six of your type won't be able to budge this truck," he said.

"Let's at least try!" The anxiety was once again in her voice, so clearly that his smile evaporated.

He walked to the door and opened it. "I'll push from here," he said, "then I can jump in if we get a bit of speed up. You try from the back." He switched the truck on, waited until she was ready at the back, and said: "Now!"

The truck moved. Just a few centimetres at first. He could hear how her shoes slipped on the grass. When he braced again, he felt them moving, and he kept on heaving and the truck kept on moving, faster, faster, until he estimated they were about half way to the creek. They were not going fast enough yet for his liking, but he jumped in and threw the truck into gear. And the first reeds on the bank were seven or eight paces away from him. He hesitated a second longer and then pressed on the accelerator and dropped the clutch, felt how the Chev jerked underneath him, and kicked in the clutch again and let go. For a moment there was nothing, except for the second jerk of the engine; then it felt as if the whole truck was trembling and the next moment the engine took. He pumped the accelerator, fast and constantly, and heard the engine miss a beat and then find a rhythm. He threw it out of gear and slammed on the brakes, put on the handbrake, still pumped the accelerator with his foot. The front wheels were in the reeds and the engine kept on missing and it seemed as if it was going to die. Out of the corner of his eye he saw the girl appear next to the window. He took his foot half way off the accelerator and held it there, then searched for reverse with the gear stick and carefully let out the clutch, felt how the truck slowly began moving backwards. He went back a little, the engine spluttering, jerking, then put it in first gear again and swung the nose right, slowly beginning to move in the direction of the sweet thorns, continually with the thought: if I can only get this thing to that incline.

But thirty paces from the sweet thorns the engine jolted and died. He kept pumping at the accelerator, but there was nothing – just the sharp smell of warm petrol.

The ensuing silence made him feel stupid.

Mália did not appear alongside the window again, and he sat and listened to the silence and suddenly knew that ever since he recognised her standing in front of his bedroom window, he had been lying to himself. He was afraid.

For a moment he wanted to think about the child and Ann. Fernando was no longer at the house; they were there alone. And he could again see his pith helmet hobbling over the veranda floor.

Delport got out and saw the girl standing behind the truck. She said nothing, just looked at him.

He listened for a moment. And everything was dead quiet. Completely. There was not even a bird chirping anywhere. He got the feeling that every stalk of grass, every bush and tree, like Mália, was watching him. And waiting for him to do something.

Pushing would not help any more. He realised it, and knew that the girl realised it as well. He assumed she was upset with him for letting the engine die, and he thought: to hell with her. But it did not make him feel any better. He was angry with himself for letting it happen; he cursed the Chev, because all of a sudden it was just as important for him to get away from the camp. And the bicycle no longer looked good enough.

He opened the bonnet and checked the battery. The earth

terminal was packed with acid residue. He pulled a few tools out from under the seat: a shifting spanner, a hammer, a screwdriver – and a hand crank.

Delport swore when he took out the hand crank.

"What's that?" the girl asked from somewhere behind him.

"Why didn't you tell me there was a ..." He could not find the Portuguese word for hand crank. "This thing," he said. "I had forgotten that you could get an engine going like this."

"Will it help?"

He began loosening the battery, did not answer, scraped the earth terminal clean with the screwdriver and tightened it on again.

"Switch on," he said and pushed the crank through the bumper, struggled to get it through the hole in the radiator. He began turning. The crank was heavy to turn and the first time he could barely move it. He took hold of it again. "Give a little petrol," he said and began cranking again, felt the engine jerk, and splutter, and cough as if it wanted to take. But when he stopped cranking, everything was quiet and he could smell the petrol again.

"Don't pump any more," he said. "Only when the engine takes." He pulled on the crank again, kept on going until his arms could go no more. His body was damp with sweat and, later, large drops fell from his nose and ran down the bumper. The engine coughed now and again, jerked, swallowed, took once, spluttered and died.

He took the spark plugs out one by one and examined them. They were not dirty. He checked the carburettor – there was petrol.

And the whole time the girl sat behind the steering wheel, watching him. Every time he looked up, he caught her eyes, and they were questioning and unsettled. But she kept quiet.

He set to the crank again, for about a minute continuously, until the muscles in his arms were sore and he could not keep it up. Then he took the crank handle out, stood up stiffly and dropped it on the ground next to him.

"We can forget about it," he said.

She climbed out.

"Get your stuff," he said. "Just not too much. I'll take you with the bike."

"Where to?"

"Albasini."

She did not ask who Albasini was.

Delport was tired. He wiped the sweat from his face with his arm, then climbed on the mudguard, grabbed the ignition coil wire and pulled it off, then took off the distributor cap and put it in his pocket. He left the key on the dashboard.

When he got to the lean-to, the girl was busy tying a bundle of clothes to the bicycle's carrier with a sash.

"They took the revolver," she said. "It was still under the pan yesterday afternoon."

He pushed the bike out from under the lean-to and walked to where the incline between the sweet thorns began; then she clambered on to the crossbar and he climbed on and for a while the bike was free-wheeling.

Then, on the flat, with the sun in their eyes, with the saddle creaking slightly under his weight, the wheels rustling in the short dry grass, he began pedalling.

They got to the path and stayed in the path as far as the creek. They went through the creek without taking off their shoes. It was already hot and they did not want to waste time.

Then he swung off the path. And they rode through the veld, due east, into the sun, in the direction of Albasini's homestead.

Delport found him where he was salting hides. He continued with his work, even when Delport came to stand beside him. Neither of them greeted the other. Only when Albasini was done spreading salt on the hide he was busy with did he nod to the worker that he could go. He stood upright with a creaking of joints and looked at Delport. They stood like that for a while, opposite each other, and Delport was suddenly no longer afraid of what he had to say.

They walked together back to the yard, and Mália was still standing in the shade next to the bike with a few inquisitive children around her; but when they saw João, they disappeared behind the house.

Delport introduced the two to each other and still said nothing by way of explanation.

A couple of chairs were standing at the back door and Albasini brought the chairs into the shade, but only the girl sat down. She kept looking at Delport as if she was expecting his eyes to tell her something.

Albasini took his pipe out and tapped it, looked at the girl and asked: "Are your people back?"

She looked up at Delport and said: "Yes."

"They haven't shot anything since they've been here," he said, "except for the pot. I thought they were looking for elephant."

"That's what they said," she said.

Albasini put his pipe into his mouth and chewed on his loose false teeth. Delport did not ask him how he knew this.

The light was sharp and somewhere was the smell of unslaked lime. Delport went to sit on the chair nearest him and asked: "Do you have place for her to stay, João? For a few days."

"We can put up a camp bed in the sitting room," Albasini said, unperturbed, the pipe still in his mouth. "What about you?"

"I'll go home."

"How long does she want to stay?"

"A day or so. Until the Mahala goes downriver again."

Delport could see the man was not comfortable. He was constantly chewing on the stem of his pipe and searched for his tobacco with a distracted hand.

He wondered how much Albasini knew.

Enough perhaps, he thought, and was relieved. He decided to say no more than what the man asked him. It was unnecessary. Besides, he was not entirely sure of anything himself; everything was vague and uncertain for him, a little incomprehensible. He would rather not try to explain anything.

"I'll have some tea made for us," Albasini said and went to the house.

"You mustn't leave me alone here," the girl said.

Delport shook his head. "I can't stay here."

"Then I'm coming with you."

"You can't."

"Well then I'm going back to the camp."

"But aren't you scared any more?"

She wanted to say something but João was on his way back to them. He came to sit beside Delport and began filling his pipe.

"Have they come to you with their permits yet?" João asked.
Delport shook his head.

"They don't have permits."

Delport looked up at the girl, saw how she turned her head
away.

"There was a falling out between her and the other two,"
Delport said, and thought: there I go already. "She wanted to get
away from there."

João nodded.

"You were the only person I could think of."

"She can stay here." João lit his pipe and between the billowing
smoke said: "If she wants to."

"I'll just go home this afternoon. I'll come and check again
tomorrow."

"Perhaps it would be better if you stayed as well," Albasini said.
Delport wanted to say something, but Albasini jumped in before
him. "I'll go round to your house tonight to say you're here. I don't
think you should go home." Delport looked up at João, but all that
he could see was a blue cloud of smoke around the man's
shoulders.

"Stay," was all the girl said.

And then neither of them spoke again, until the tea arrived.
Tombi brought it and put the tray down on the ground next to
João without greeting them, then quietly disappeared.

Delport thought: I do not want to stay here – I must go home.
But he said nothing, just drank his tea, waited. He was agitated.
He kept an eye on the yard, on the trees around the house. He
thought: I'm not afraid – why should I be afraid? I've got nothing
to do with any of this. This is none of my business. I don't know
these people. It's their mess. Why should I be afraid?

Albasini drank his tea slowly and that made Delport
impatient. He watched Albasini, and looked at the lazy chickens
in the yard which were walking and picking at the ground in
the sharp light, listened to the children talking in the house.
But he avoided Mália Domingo's eyes. He felt he had done his
duty with her, he was finished with her – she had to look after
herself from here on. But, nevertheless, he was afraid of
meeting her eyes, afraid it would make him change his mind,

because he could still feel her back against his chest and her hair against his chin while they struggled uncertainly through the low grass, without talking, with the bike's saddle and the dry chain protesting and the sun ever heavier on them and over the desolate veld and the silence constantly like a question mark between the two of them. He recalled her warm back and how defenceless she was while washing her body in the first light that morning.

He wondered how it must feel to hold a gun in your hands and to really care, to hold a gun – perhaps a machine-gun: that would be much easier, a machine-gun – and to stand upright, to know it is important enough, it really matters, and to pull the trigger, to feel how the trigger trembles against your finger, and to rattattattattattattattat over the patch of shining yard and into the grey Chev and the tent, and the Mahala's hull and to shred the six white letters and the storeroom, at the pane with the green stain, every windowpane, every door, the rats in the ceiling, the Makonde mask with the hump and the mbira, the lanterns and the half-empty whisky bottle, to rattattattattat, everyone in front of him, everything, the stinkweed, the child's roads, the damned sun itself, and the cicadas, Fernando, the bicycle's saddle, Mália, the scratching chickens and the tray, Albasini, to rattattattattat, to rattattattattat, for their sake, for everyone's sake, until he was clean. Completely clean.

And then to go and sleep. Just to sleep. To sleep.

But he knew he would never get that far. He would never have the courage; he would never dare. He would just stand, and wait, watch what happens, watch what happens to him. He would not lift a finger; everything is inception, everything is beginning, and he no longer sees the possibility of beginning. However: doing nothing, he thought, can also be a cause. Doing nothing could make him more guilty than with a machine-gun.

He looked at Albasini and wondered what Albasini thought. Then lifted his hands to look at his nails and the movement gave him a fright. He sat dead still and looked beyond his nails to the edge of the yard, at the house, and listened to how the children talked and laughed somewhere. He looked at his fingernails without moving his hands or his head. The ten fingernails stared back at him like blind eyes; each one multiplied and became ten eyes that watched and listened all at the same time.

Then Albasini put his cup down and called over his shoulder for Tombi. Delport did not hear her approaching, but after a short while she was next to him and Albasini said: "This is Dona Domingo. She's sleeping here tonight. You must make a bed for her in the sitting room." Tombi nodded and Delport could see how the black woman looked stiffly at Mália and bent over and picked up the tray. "She'll go with you," Albasini said. "Show her the house and bring her some water; she'll want to wash."

Only then did Delport look at the girl and her eyes were uncertainly on his, for a moment, and he looked away.

Tombi hesitated and Delport could feel the sudden tension between the two women. The black woman waited for the white to stand up, she did not want to invite her.

"Go with her," João said to the girl and Tombi turned around and walked away, and only a few moments later did Mália stand up and follow her quickly.

"You must stay here tonight," said João.

Delport asked: "Why?"

"It's safer here, *amigo*."

"So what do you know about them?" Delport asked.

Albasini shook his head.

"You know something," Delport said.

"I don't know anything." Then Albasini stood up and raised his eyebrow at Delport in passing. They walked round the back of the house, past the shrivelled lemon tree with the limp sweet blossoms. There was the shell of a rusted truck on blocks in the furthest corner of the yard and the mudguards and roof were white from dry chicken droppings. They went to lean against it and Albasini said: "You must go with her when the Mahala sails."

"And what about Ann and the child?" Delport asked.

"You must decide about them for yourself."

Delport kept his eye on Albasini when he said: "I don't trust that girl, João."

But the older man only blew a cloud of smoke into the air as if dismissing the mistrust with that, and said: "Just stay here."

"Why are you so worried about me?"

Albasini looked at him and said: "Why are you worried about Ann and them?"

"He was apparently at the house. Twice. While I was out in the veld."

"Perhaps he was looking for you."

"He knew I wasn't there."

Albasini turned around and slowly began walking away; Delport followed him. They walked between the tall candelabra trees and Delport looked up at the yellow, fleshy arms of the tree and heard flies somewhere between the sickly blossoms. Then he heard João ask: "Who is that chap, exactly?"

Delport looked over the yard, and there was no one to be seen. The yard was bare, silent; it lay hard and hot, baking under the sun and a few poinsettia and wild pawpaws stood tiredly in the sharp midday sun and waited for the evening.

"I don't know," Delport said and came to a stop.

"Are you sure?"

"No."

Then Albasini put his pipe in his pocket and walked away through the trees, suddenly in a hurry, in the direction of the camps.

Delport did not follow him. He looked towards the house, as if he was expecting the girl somewhere, and after a while he could see her standing at a window. She was standing and watching him and made him hope that she stayed where she was. He went into the shade of the candelabra trees and listened to the flies. There was a large chameleon on one of the trunks, yellow-green and perfectly still, that slowly turned its beady eyes, keeping watch on the yard, and on Delport, almost completely camouflaged.

When Delport looked at the window again, between the peeling tree trunks, the girl was no longer there. She was standing in front of the house, uncertain, and looked in the direction of where he had been a moment before.

He went further into the trees and heard the flies droning deep in the tough blossoms like wind blowing in the distance. And he went even deeper into the trees, stood briefly, listened, and after a while saw the girl standing, near him, in the place where the chameleon was. But she was looking in another direction.

He did not want to go any further, but he moved a few paces to the right, between the umbrella thorns, and stood still, certain that she could not see him, and wished he could get to his bicycle, leave without anyone seeing him. He wanted to go home. He was tired of drifting along together on a river of events that had nothing to do with him. He was tired of dancing to someone else's tune. He was tired of staring at nothing.

He was dog tired from dying. He wanted to get to his bike and go. But there were footsteps somewhere and the girl appeared through the branches and came to stand near him.

"You mustn't be afraid," she said.

"I'm not scared."

"You must trust me." The tone of her voice made him think again of that afternoon in Caipemba when she had come to him between all the flies. He heard her ask again, self-conscious at her predicament: "Do you know how much it costs? To the third stop?"

"I do trust you," he said.

She stood and looked at him, but he was sure she did not see him, she saw something behind him. He heard her say: "I want to help you."

"How?" he asked.

"Do you know who Bvekenya is?"

He shook his head. "Who is he?"

"I don't know."

And she came up to him and began unbuttoning his shirt. He could smell her: she smelled like the red handkerchief in his room. Carefully she undid the buttons on his shirt, very carefully, and kept on looking at him, then rubbed her hands over his chest, down his sides, and pressed her cheek against his body. "I can hear your heart," she said. She pushed her hands into his shirt and ran them over his back.

He wanted to push her away from him, but his hands stayed resting large and dead on her body and there were too many cicadas and he recalled the chameleon's beady eyes. Then her hand was somewhere between them and he saw how she undid the buttons on her shirt, one by one, quickly, until her breasts were naked against his sweaty body and the nipples hard against his skin.

"You can take me," she said, her voice anxious again like that morning. "Take me, please, take me, and forget about him, he doesn't have a name."

Her lips were wet against his skin, and slightly open; he could feel every word against his body. He could feel her teeth; she bit him gently and held him and he knew she was scared. But he turned around, away from her, and somewhere in the trees heard a honey-guide whistle.

There was a small round hole in the gauze. He could see it clearly.

"I'm going now," he said.

"Where to?"

"I'm going home."

He walked back to the house, past the shell of the truck, past the struggling lemon tree. He heard a child crying in the house and when he went past a window, Tombi and Tanda were talking lazily and in whispers behind the hot windowpanes.

Delport took his bike and began pushing it towards the path. But João Albasini called from a distance. He could not see him – it was just his voice somewhere between the trees, behind the cicadas. He was not sure whether he should pay attention to Albasini, but after a while realised his bike's front wheel was not turning any longer, the bike leaned unmoving against him. He stood and waited, and knew Mália Domingo hesitated three paces from him, behind him, scared and close to him.

It all felt very familiar to him. While the afternoon passed by, every event, every gesture, every word that was said, every turn seemed like a memory. And everything was so far away from him, like memories, and everything that he wanted to prevent or change, continued unchangeable on its path like something that was already past.

Albasini came to stand beside him and asked: "What are you doing now, *amigo*?"

"I'm going."

"Where to?"

"Does it matter?"

"You can take my motorbike," Albasini said after a while.

"I don't want your motorbike."

"Take the motorbike."

Then the girl appeared at his other side. "Take the motorbike," she said. "I'll go with you."

"My bike is good enough." Delport wanted to leave again.

"You can get there faster on the motorbike."

"Who says I want to get there faster?"

"Albasini pushed his large pith helmet back on his head, chewed on his loose false teeth, just stood for a while, and looked at Delport.

"I know where you're headed," the girl said. Delport did not answer, and the girl said: "You're going back to the camp."

Delport did not answer. He was not sure all of a sudden and he was not in a hurry to decide. He would come to a decision along the way, he thought.

Then he heard Albasini say: "Look at the weather. Damn."

There was a change coming. It would rain that night, perhaps even before dark. There was a bank of clouds in the east, and the air was still and muggy.

Delport thought: perhaps she is right: perhaps I am going back to the camp.

Then he started pushing his bike, quickly, and swung his leg over the saddle, and rode, through the yard to the road, and down the road.

"*Amigo!*" he heard João calling from behind. "*Amigo* – you mustn't!" He rode on, and heard João calling from ever further away, and did not look round or listen. It was two o'clock in the afternoon and too early for rain, but the rain was near. The air was as heavy as lead and dead still; he could feel himself riding through the air.

And he was in a hurry to get home.

9

The yard and the house seemed as if they had been suddenly abandoned. He called their names through the wire gauze, through the windows. But there was nothing. No one. And when the rain broke over the roof, he sat in the sitting room, under the buffalo head, with the gun next to him, and drank the last of the whisky.

It was six o'clock.

Soon it was dark and he imagined that he heard someone above the droning of the rain. He wanted to look out of the window, but he could not see anything – only fleetingly saw, when the lightning splintered over the yard, the ridges on the tank, the pawpaw tree, the storeroom's sickly green door. Then he turned around, and the lightning was there again, a blue flash, and in that split second he saw Ritter's face, against the wall, under the buffalo head. The empty glass was in his hand and he could hear, a moment later, how it broke against the man's forehead, and how the mask fell.

Then he was outside in the warm rain with the gun in his hands and the lightning continuously around him, dancing over the yard, and he ran and in the blue light he could see the child's roads winding around the bougainvilleas and between the banana trees.

His bicycle was against the kitchen wall. He hung the gun over his shoulder and took his bike. Only then did he see that the girl's clothes were still on the carrier. He pushed the bike away and climbed on, rode into the darkness, away from the yard, to the path, and past the servants' quarters. His clothes were sopping wet. He could feel the water running down his cheeks and back, but the rain was warm and there was not much wind. It felt to him as if it was sweat running over him.

At Dois creek the rain eased off a little, and only as he pushed his bike through the water did he realise for the first time that he still had the gun, and wondered why he had brought it. It made no sense.

If it is Ritter, he thought, if Ritter is waiting for him at the camp, if he leaves his bike against the mahogany's trunk and turns around and sees Ritter standing beside the truck or in the opening to the tent – what will he do with the gun? Should he shoot? Or should he wait for Ritter to take his hand out of the pocket of his bush jacket.

He took the gun off his shoulder and opened the magazine, took the bullets out and threw them one by one into the darkness, afraid that he would later change his mind. Then he put the gun down in the grass and pushed the bike up the slippery bank of the creek as far as where it levelled out. And rode.

There was a moment when he did hesitate. He rode past the place where they had found Gonçalo. He recalled the small hole above the native's eye again and was sorry about the gun. In front of him in the rain, a hammerhead flew out of the heavy grass and rowed away in the darkness. He rode more slowly, and there was a moment when he wanted to stop – but he was afraid of stopping; he was afraid of turning back. He knew: as soon as he stopped the bike, he would turn back, even though he knew he would never forgive himself for it.

He wanted to see Ritter. He wanted to see those eyes again that bore into him and he wanted to say: "Evening, Ritter. I've come. I wasn't afraid." He would lean his bike against the tree. Perhaps it would be raining again by then. It would be dark. He would turn around from his bike and perhaps there would be a little lightning. Then he would know – that was the moment for which he had waited for something like a lifetime – he would see Ritter standing near him in the blue light. And he would say: "Evening, Ritter."

He said it aloud while riding. While the rain had begun falling again, soft and warm on his face, from high in the darkness, he said aloud, just to feel the words, just to know how it would fit in his mouth: "Evening, Ritter. I've come."

It was not raining hard. Perhaps it was just that he was used to the rain by then. He was only aware of it sometimes. He listened to the krrrr-click of the dry chain, to the chirping saddle, and tried to forget about the strange silence of the yard and about the child's roads and Ann's bed. The rain on the dark veld was a monotonous, gentle sound, like a constant whispering.

After a while he went into the sweet thorns and here and there he had to duck for the low, rain-laden branches. Later he had to get off the bike and push. But as the trees began to thin out again and the path to open, he did not ride again. He pushed the bike. He was tired.

Then the grey truck was in front of him in the grass.

He went past the truck to the tent, thirty paces further, and leaned his bike against the wet trunk of the mahogany tree, and turned around. He could hear the rain sifting down on the tent, but he could barely see the tent. He stood and waited for the lightning or for a voice, a movement, a footstep somewhere in the grass. But there was nothing, absolutely nothing except the lonely sound of the rain.

He walked around the tent, stood again and listened and then walked through the grass to the truck. The flap was closed and he hit against it gently a few times with his hand. There was no reaction. "Is anyone here?" he asked and hit the canvas again. Then he walked around to the front of the truck. The seat was still askew as he had left it, and the driver's door was slightly open.

There were nightjars in the dip; he could hear their unsettled screaming and it was a sickly and lonely sound. He kept watching the dip and they kept on screaming, and later he could see them flutter up from out of the dull grass and swarm off over the hulking trees.

He went back to the tent and looked for a place in one corner where he could open the flap, but suddenly dropped his hands. A mug or something fell over inside the tent.

"Roberto?" he heard the girl ask quietly inside the tent. He could hear she was scared.

He waited.

"Roberto, is that you?" And then, after a while, more quietly, more unsure: "Delport?"

"Yes."

A few moments went by before she said: "*Entra!*"

He looked for the loose end of the flap again, pulled it open and went inside.

It was dark inside. He could not see her and he stood still, his fingers still holding the flap, and said: "Evening."

"Evening."

He could hear from her voice that she was close to him, to his right.

"Why don't you get some light?"

"I was scared."

"Do you have matches?"

"I've only got a blanket on," she said. "My clothes are wet." He remained standing.

"You took my dry clothes away with you. On the back of your bike."

"They're also wet."

"Why did you come back?" she asked. "You shouldn't have."

"I didn't know you'd be here."

"I couldn't stay there. I didn't want to."

He sighed and moved forward, touched a chair, turned it round and felt it and sat down.

"Was nobody here?" he asked eventually.

"No."

"Did you walk here?"

"No. He brought me."

"João?"

"Yes."

He heard her behind him, felt her touch him. And he was scared. All of a sudden he was not sure if it was her that was touching him. But when he felt her hand on his head, he was sure it was her. She put her hand on his shoulder and said: "You're wet."

"I'm tired," he said.

"Where were you?"

"I think I was at the house."

"Why did you come back?"

"There is no one at the house any more."

162

"Have they left?"

He could see Ann lying under the mosquito net.

When she spoke again, her face was near his head. He could feel her breath on his cheek. "Are you scared?" she asked.

"Yes."

"But you came back?"

"Yes."

"Why?"

"I wanted to make sure."

"Of what?"

He thought for a while, tried to think, and then said: "I can't believe that I really had something to do with all of these things."

"Perhaps you did."

"But I didn't do anything."

"That doesn't matter."

"Really?"

"I don't know."

It was raining hard, but while they talked, he tried to listen to see if he could not perhaps hear something above the sound of the rain.

"I talk," he said. "I'm continually trying to explain why I did this or that, and the whole time I know I'm just trying to explain because I – because it was me who did it. One should probably know why one did certain things. But I..."

"You really don't know."

"No."

The rain came and went; sometimes it was deafening and sometimes it was just a fine whisper on the tent. When it was raining very hard, they did not talk, just listened to the sound.

"I don't really understand it," he said at one point.

"What?"

"You must explain everything to me again. Right from the very start."

"About me?"

"About both of us. And about Bvekenya. About everything. Tell me everything again right from the very start."

"Why?" she asked.

"I got confused somewhere along the line."

She did not answer, but after a while he could hear her moving in the dark. He could hear the matches and then there was a yellow flame in the darkness; he could see her hand, the corner of the blanket, her eyes as she brought the lantern closer and lifted the glass up and lit the wick. The light grew softly and brown around them and she pulled the blanket tightly around her and went to sit on the other chair at the opposite corner of the table. The table was next to him and he let his arm rest on it.

She did not look at him.

His hand was brown and dead in the scarce light and his nails were dull.

"Let's play," she said.

"What?"

"Let's pretend there is no one else."

"How do you play that?"

"Just like you play anything else," she said. "It's easy to play."

"I've already seen," he said, "how easy it is for you."

She looked at him, and her face was soft in the light. He could see the lantern's light reflected in her eyes.

"You pretended you were innocent and lonely and left in the lurch."

"At first I pretended and then I stopped. I got scared."

"And now you want to pretend again."

"No."

"You want to pretend there is no one else."

She kept quiet and said nothing.

"Tell me about him," he said. "About Bvekenya."

"What must I tell?"

"Is he old?"

She looked away and said: "I don't know how old he is."

"He must be close to fifty."

"He's older," she said, her face still turned away. "You won't know him. He lost his one leg and he struggles to walk, and he doesn't see very well any more."

"Ritter?"

"I don't know who Ritter is," she said and suddenly looked at him again. "I'm talking about Bvekenya."

"He has long yellow hair that sometimes hangs over his..."

She shook her head.

"No?"

"He's almost got no hair." She stroked her hand over the back of her head. "Just a little grey hair here."

They kept quiet and listened to the rain, looked at each other. Later she stood up; there was a tarpaulin on the ground and she went to sit on it and pulled the blanket tighter around her.

Moths were gathering around the lantern's hot glass; they came out of the tarpaulin's folds, out from under the table, and flickered around the light, around the blackened kettle and the dirty mugs on the table, around their faces.

"There's another blanket on my chair," she said, "if you're getting cold."

He pushed both of his arms across the table. There were still a few isolated, glistening drops in the hair on his wrists. "Do you think they'll still come?" he asked.

"I don't know."

Then he turned the lantern down and rested his head on his arms. And listened to the rain.

He dreamed he saw the yard and the house. The pawpaw tree was dead still in the rain and loose shoots of the bougainvilleas hung low under the heavy drops. The radio repeated the signature tune again and again – he could hear it at the storeroom and behind the kitchen; monotonous, like the narina trogon's whining call, somewhere out of the wilderness of Africa. He listened to the signature tune and saw the green stain in the windowpane, and the small Makonde figure staggering under the balled fist of its dark hump, slightly bow-legged over the eleven carved Swahili words that Rodrigues so diligently deciphered. "We are two. I and me. We wrestle together. To death." Four sentences: the first three equal in length; three words each, and the fourth two words. He was sitting at the table on the back veranda and watched the centipede sitting above the doorframe, a few centimetres away from the peeling plaster. Ann came out of the dark sitting room and appeared in the doorway and there was blood on her crinkled slip. She wanted to talk with him, but she could not.

Then he was in the tent and he was lying with the girl and both of them were without clothes. And someone opened the tent's flap. It was light outside and he could see Ritter in the opening. He looked completely different. He struggled to balance with his walking stick; his skin was very brown and tough as leather and his face was full of fine wrinkles. He was a small man and skinny and his long hair was thin and grey.

He wanted to talk to Ritter, but he could not. He saw how Ritter pulled a sword out from his belt and the sun shimmered briefly on the shiny blade – only fleetingly, like lightning. He began throwing bullets at Ritter, flinging them one by one at his forehead. They bounced off his forehead and Ritter did not blink once.

Later, when he woke up, there was only a small blue flame on the lamp's wick. When he tried turning it, it flickered for a while and then died.

He looked for the matches, but heard her say somewhere in the darkness: "The oil's finished."

"Aren't you sleeping?"

"No."

"Is there more oil?"

"In the truck."

He listened and it was still raining.

"Why don't you sleep?" he asked.

"You're not sleeping either."

He stood up and stretched. The tent flap was closed and it was stuffy. But his body was stiff and his clothes damp on his back and his legs.

The nightjars were still somewhere in the rain, nearby, and he wondered what was making them so unsettled. When, later, he opened the flap and looked out, part of the sky was clear and it was cooler outside; the night was clear and he could feel a slight breeze, coming from between the trees.

He stood in the opening and listened to the creek, to the nightjars, and thought of Ann, of the child, of the girl trying to sleep on the ground behind him. The grey truck's roof glinted slightly from the rain and the little light the night reflected.

It will not come to anything, he thought. The night will pass and the sun will rise. It will be a clear day and the birds will sing and perhaps there will be impala in the dip grazing in the early morning and later they will go and drink below the flat rocks and he will no longer know why he had expected something.

The rain fell more finely and, after a while, he went out and stood in the rain and listened to see if he could hear anything. He could hear the creek. He thought: the water will be in the river with the sunrise, in a week's time it will flow into the sea and disappear, change – no one will recognise it any longer. It will follow the same route by which he came to be here; it will be lifted from the great morass out of which Ritter had come dripping that night in Ballito.

Delport walked away from the tent and stood among the shadows and listened to the drops from leaves. He recalled Ann lying under the mosquito net, soaked with sweat, her hands clutched between her knees. And the child looking mistrustfully at him, then turning around, disappearing in the darkness, and laughing softly from a distance. The child in the dark next to the mosquito net standing and staring at the pale, writhing body between the sheets, screaming and grabbing on to her shoulders.

He stood outside for a long time, until the leaves barely dripped any more, and there was nothing to see – where the sky in the north had earlier been clearing, the night had begun closing in again and the few lone stars disappeared one by one. Until it was completely dark and he had to search for the tent. He walked into a chair and stood still. Then he lifted the tent flap and asked: "*Que horas são?*"

"I don't know," she said.

He bent over and felt around in the dark, touched her face.

"You must sleep," she said.

He sat on his haunches, next to her.

"Will they still come?" he asked.

"I don't know."

He lay down on the tarpaulin, on his stomach, with his chin on his arms, and looked out of the flap into the darkness. And she groaned softly and rolled over on to her back up against him, her head on his elbow.

Then he said: "Mália."

He could feel how she turned her head slowly to him.

167

"What are we going to do if they don't come?"

"They'll come."

"When?"

"I don't know."

He closed his eyes and felt the ground swaying very slowly under him.

Later, she stood up and he could hear her pouring water and drinking it. Then she came to lie with him again.

They lay a long time like that and listened to how the night became quieter, and even quieter, until later it was just their breathing. He could still feel the ground swaying slightly under him; it was as if the ground and the darkness were swaying together. He put his hands under the blanket and stroked her, over her hip and her shoulder, over her arm, over the soft side of her breast, and felt he was drifting on something, drifting away from her, away from his own body, until he was somewhere up near the roof of the tent and could look down on himself and on her where they were lying together in the darkness.

She said: "Try to love me."

And he waited for something in him to offer an answer, but his hands were heavy and he could not think.

"There's nothing else," she said.

His lips were in her hair and he could feel the shape of her skull with them. "Why did you come here?" his lips asked her. "In the beginning."

"Try to hold me," she said. "Hold me and don't ask, please. Don't think. Don't be scared."

"I don't really know why you came."

"It's not important."

"I want to tell you about Ritter," he said. "Have I told you about him yet?"

"Tell me about yourself."

"They're exactly the same."

"Tell me then. Just keep talking. I don't want to sleep, I just want to listen to you. I want to hear what you have to say."

"I want to tell you about Ritter."

"Tell me about him."

"I did love her."

There was still not a sign of light anywhere. The day still seemed far off and there was nothing to tell.

"I thought it would be incredibly easy. I knew nothing about being in love."

"Hold me," she said.

"We often laid like this at night and talked and sometimes just laid quietly and waited and we didn't know why we were waiting. I did not want to go away then. I did not want the child to be taken away. I did not know why I had to run away from anybody. I didn't want to. I did not want to be here tonight. I don't know why I'm here."

She lay perfectly still and after a while said: "You're not talking."

"What do you think happened to him?" he asked.

She did not answer.

The child lay outside on the patch of lawn and there was a round hole in the stretched wire gauze of Ann's bedroom door. She was lying on her back and the sheet was thrown back, away from her body. He could see the dark mark on her breast and her arm hung down from the bed.

"Are you asleep?" he asked.

She did not answer. She lay perfectly still and her body was cold.

"The wind's beginning to blow outside," he said. "Aren't you getting cold?"

The rain had completely gone and he could hear her breathing, softly, like the flutter of a moth's wing. The creek was a monotonous gurgling outside and, now and again, a drop fell from the heavy leaves on to the tent.

He lay and waited and saw how the light began drawing lines on the treetops systematically; first, only vaguely – and, later, ever more clearly. And eventually he could make out the patchwork in the roof of the tent. And the girl sighed sometimes, sometimes moved a little, and then slept on.

Then, with the light already a little grey, he fell asleep again and in his sleep heard redbuck whistling, heard the wind moving outside in the grass. And when he woke up, it was lighter, but there was mist between the trees and he could see the back wheel of his bicycle.

The child lay on the patch of lawn where he was busy making a road. The small plank was still in his hand and his one leg was drawn up a little against his body as if he was trying to shield himself. There was a round hole in the gauze of Ann's door, one metre above the floor, and a hole in the twisted mosquito net, and in line with the two holes a red spot on her breast, above the stained sheet. Her hand hung down from the bed.

She was still asleep when he got up. It was cold and his body was stiff in his damp clothes. He stretched and in the tent opening sank to his haunches, looked down at the shining trail of an earthworm that patiently, slimily crept over the ground.

He thought: that's the third sign.

The mist was white in the dip and the trees drifted heavily and lazily, like dead birds. He went down to the creek and washed his hands and face, thinking: first there was the chameleon on the candelabra tree – that was the first sign; then the hammerhead that flew up out of the grass; the earthworm was the third sign.

Then he walked back, past the tent, into the trees. His eyes were sandy from too little sleep, and where the mist had lifted, he turned around and stood and watched the sun coming up.